A NOVEL

By C. L. Cattano

Cursed Hearts

A Vagary Publishing Book

Copyright © 2011, 2016 by C. L. Cattano

Cover Art, Title Page Art and Typesetting Copyright © 2016 by Chynsia Hinesley

Published by:

VAGARY PUBLISHING

www.vagarypublishing.com
inquiry@vagarypublishing.com

Rogena Mitchell-Jones, Independent Literary Editor
RMJ Manuscript Services LLC *www.rogenamitchell.com*
Proofreading by AmiLynn Hadley

Printed by CreateSpace

Fonts used in this book: Body – Adobe Garamond Pro, Headings – AR Christy.

ISBN 978-0-9980906-1-0
First Edition
10 9 8 7 6 5 4 3 2 1

AcKNoWLedgeMeNtS

I WOULD LIKE to thank everyone involved in making this completed project happen from editing to artwork to just listening to me go on and on about the whole thing. Without you and the help and encouragement you gave, the process would not have been such a great journey.

To all of you I give my deep appreciation and thanks.

Dedication

For Marie who did not snooze…

Picture this:
It starts before we even kiss.
We feel the connection,
before either of us touches the other one.
A bond of pure emotion
has captured us, though separated by time.
An overpowering yearning of the heart,
time and distance have failed to keep apart.
There is no release from this web of ardor,
woven by the Fates with threads of the future.

Chapter 1

KNIVES, MEAT, AND guts were strewn across the kitchen table and dripping onto the floor. Jessie took in the gory scene with horror and softly gasped as she watched the culprit stand over the slimy mess with a large, sharp, gleaming knife. She watched quietly until she gained some control over her emotions as the culprit cut and slashed with manic determination.

"What the hell are you doing?" Jessie asked as calmly as she could as she watched the sharp knife come down on the soft flesh and then make a sucking sound as it was pulled free.

The offender looked up in surprise at Jessie's outburst and gave her a menacing grin while holding the shining knife in the air, poised for another plunge into the firm but yielding flesh. "Stop right there! Don't come any closer!"

Jessie put her hand to her mouth and shook her head in disbelief. "Louise! Just how many fucking pumpkins did you buy?"

Louise looked up innocently at Jessie and quickly dropped the knife to her side. "Well, I've got thirteen."

"Thirteen? Thirteen! Why the hell did you have to get thirteen pumpkins?" Jessie fumed.

"Now, Jess, don't be mad. This is our first Halloween together, and I just wanted to do things right," Louise explained.

"Do things right? Look at this mess! I hope you know I'm not helping you clean it up!"

Louise looked around at the messy kitchen and laughed. "I did kind of make a big mess."

"Kind of?" Jessie snapped as she put her hands on her hips and rolled her eyes.

"Yeah, that's why I warned you not to come all the way in. I didn't want you to slip on the guts or anything." Louise smiled charmingly.

"Oh, well, in that case. I'm still not helping you clean it up!" Jessie snapped as she turned and stormed out of the kitchen.

Louise grinned as she watched Jessie walk out. She began quickly making an effort to clean the kitchen as well as Jessie would have. Louise knew she would never get it clean enough for her, but she would try. God, she loved that woman.

Finally, Louise got the kitchen back into some sort of order and went to look for Jessie. She grinned when she found her sitting on the bed putting on her after-shower lotion that smelled so good. She slipped into the room, sat next to Jessie, and began helping smooth the cream over her.

"Lou, stop," said Jessie as she pushed Louise's hand off her leg. "You've got sticky pumpkin gunk all over you, and I just took a shower."

"I know, and you smell good, and you feel good," Louise purred as she stole a kiss and pushed her back on the bed.

"Umph, Lou! Stop! I can smell the pumpkin, and believe me, it doesn't smell good!"

Louise laughed as she pulled away grabbing Jessie's hands and pulling her up with her. "Well, then, I guess you'll have to come back into the shower and make sure I get clean enough for you."

Jessie gave a small laugh as Louise pulled her into her embrace and began kissing her and pushing off her robe. "My god. Don't you ever think about anything but sex?"

Louise chuckled. "Yes, but only when you're not around."

"Oh, so it's only when I'm around that you think about sex?"

"Yeah," Louise whispered heavily into Jessie's ear pulling her into the shower and turning on the water. "I'm so glad you already took a shower."

"You are?" Jessie breathed out heavily as Louise kissed that one spot on her neck that made her lose control. "Wh—why?"

Louise moved her kisses back up to Jessie's ear. "Water's already warm."

Jessie moaned softly as the warm water ran over her body and Louise's kisses covered her neck and breasts. She felt Louise's confident hands run over her, pulling her closer as they kissed under the falling water. Leaning against the cool tile, Jessie arched her back as Louise made her way down her body and spread her legs. Louise worked her tongue around and into Jessie, tasting her and slowly licking her in wide circles and long, lingering strokes. Jessie held Louise's head as the ache building inside her caused her to let out a quiet moan. She was so wet for Louise that even the water could not wash it away. Louise slid her fingers inside her, thrusting gently and teasing her swollen clit with her tongue as the steam surrounded them, and the sound of the water was lost in their passion.

———————

IN THE WARMTH of their bed, Louise lay quietly in Jessie's embrace listening to her heartbeat. Jessie played with a fine lock of

Louise's auburn hair as she willed her body to keep the sensation that Louise had caused inside her.

"I'm glad you only think about sex when I'm here," she declared suddenly.

Louise tried to hold in a laugh, but she failed. Her body made the bed shake with its release. "Really?"

"Don't laugh," she said losing her battle at looking serious. "Yes, I am."

"Why's that?"

"Oh, because."

Louise sat up and leaned over Jessie. "Because? Oh, because. I get it. Because you love me, right?"

Jessie nodded her head and smiled. "I'm glad we understand each other. Yes, because I love you."

Louise gave Jessie a sweet, slow, deep kiss and then pulled away slightly. "I love you too," she whispered.

"I hope so." Jessie sighed as their kiss continued.

"I do. I'll always love you. I love you unconditionally."

"Unconditionally?"

Louise kissed Jessie deeply again and ran her hand over her body as she nodded her head. "And you'll love me always too, right? Always?"

Jessie closed her eyes as Louise kissed her neck and shoulder. "Right, always." She sighed at the sensation.

"Good," Louise breathed softly as she moved her hand between Jessie's legs.

Jessie opened her eyes and frowned as she looked down at the top of Louise's head. "Good? Why good?"

Louise continued kissing and caressing Jessie as she gave a slight shrug. "No reason. It's just good."

Jessie put her hand over her face. "Fuck!" She pressed her hand to her forehead as she felt Louise's warm fingers move through her. "Louise, you left a mess in the kitchen, didn't you?" She could feel Louise's breath on her breast, and her tongue circling her nipple as her fingers entered her slightly then slid slowly back up to her clit. Her mind wanted to wring Louise's neck, but she was so wet now, and her body was in beautiful torment from her touch. "Oh, fuck it," she moaned. "How do you do this to me?"

Louise made her way back up to Jessie's lips and filled her mouth with her tongue and kissed her breathlessly. "I love you. Very, very much."

Chapter 2

THE MORNING SUN shined through the kitchen window as Jessie grumbled under her breath. "Damn it, Lou! Takes me all fucking morning to clean up your mess, and where the hell are you? Who knows?" she shouted to the empty kitchen as she spread a thick layer of newspaper over one end of the table and placed the last un-carved pumpkin on it. At the moment, it was probably a good thing Louise had to leave for an early morning photo shoot in Central Park.

"There. At least, this time, the mess will be under some sort of control." She turned back to the sink and began scrubbing the soaking knives that were covered with dried pumpkin guts. The soapy water had softened the mess, and she was able to clean them easier. "She has got to start paying more attention to what she's doing," Jessie complained to herself as she scrubbed the cutlery. "She just goes fucking manic with her crazy projects and leaves a fucking mess every time! It's like living with a child!"

She looked over at the row of pumpkins by the back door and sighed. Each one was cut differently with its own personality that somehow seemed to fit the pumpkin perfectly.

Jessie could not help smiling as she remembered the surprise on Louise's face when she interrupted her. Louise was concentrating so intently on her project that she didn't hear the front door open or notice that she was watching her. She stood at the door for the longest time just watching her work—and making a mess.

Looking out the kitchen window, Jessie saw Louise getting out of her car with a large shopping bag and a huge silly grin on her face. She shook her head and turned her attention back to the cutlery.

"Like living with a child," she mumbled.

"So you want children?" Louise asked as she entered the room.

"No, I don't want children. I have you!" Jessie smirked.

Louise laughed and gave her a quick kiss. "Yes, you do." She sat her shopping bag on the table and looked at the pumpkin sitting on the newspaper. "What's this?"

"That is how you don't make a huge mess when you carve a pumpkin."

"Oh. Well, that's the thirteenth pumpkin. You never carve the thirteenth pumpkin."

"Of course." Jessie sighed. "Everyone knows that!" she added sarcastically. "So what exactly do you do with the thirteenth pumpkin? Oh, better question, why is it we *need* thirteen pumpkins?"

Louise began pulling candles and little jars from the shopping bag and winked at Jessie. "You'll see. I'll explain everything very soon."

"I can't wait," Jessie said dryly as she put the knives back in the knife block.

Louise slid up behind Jessie and put her arms around her, kissed her neck, then whispered, "I know. But you'll just have to wait."

Jessie closed her eyes as Louise's kisses melted her frustrations away. She rotated toward Louise and returned the kisses. Her heart beat hard in her chest as a warm tingling sensation ran through her body. "My, god, I love you," she moaned into Louise's mouth.

"Mmm, I love you, too. Thank you for doing all this. I did try, you know."

"I know you did. You always do," Jessie admitted.

"I've got something for you," Louise whispered as she continued to kiss Jessie softly.

Jessie smiled and kissed Louise back. "What?" She looked at Louise's big grin, which caused her to frown, and she began to worry. "Lou, you better not have gotten me a big rubber spider or anything slimy!"

Louise doubled over with laughter and pulled away to get into the bag on the table. "No, I didn't get you anything like that." She pulled out a small ornately tooled leather box and presented it to Jessie in the palm of her hand. "Happy Halloween."

Jessie looked suspiciously at the box sitting innocently in her hand. She hesitated for a moment then carefully picked it up, a bit unnerved by the sparkle in Louise's eyes. She carefully opened the hinged top of the box and was relieved when nothing happened. She looked inside the box, and her eyes widened with surprise, as she saw nestled inside was a beautiful antique pendant.

"Do you like it?" asked Louise, who was getting a bit nervous as Jessie just stared at the pendant.

"Oh, my god, Lou! I love it!" She looked up to see Louise's relieved face and shook her head in wonder. "Why? Why are you giving me this? I thought we agreed to no gifts, and we were just going to spend time together for our anniversary tomorrow. I… I didn't get anything for you. I didn't know."

Louise took the pendant and slipped it over Jessie's head. "Because I love you. I've had the pendant at the studio for a long time. I had to go get a new chain for it this morning. You don't have to get me anything. You're my gift. The things you do for me, the fact that you love me—that's all I need."

Jessie looked down sadly. "Oh, great!"

"What?"

"Oh, now I feel like a shit. I've been complaining about you all morning and about the mess I've had to clean up, and now you do this." She looked at the pendant again then into Louise's eyes. "I do love you. This is so beautiful, thank you." She gave Louise a sweet and loving kiss hoping that she could feel just how much she really did love her through her kiss.

<hr>

LOUISE HAD FINISHED marking places around the house where she wanted to set all of the pumpkins and then taking them out to their places one by one. As she worked, she was thinking of Jessie and how much their love for each other had grown over the past year. She could not get enough of her. Haunted—that's what she was, haunted by the love she felt inside for her. She carried her with her everywhere and could not bring herself to put her down. She could not release her. She felt as if Jessie's power over her was supernatural. She could snatch the very thoughts out of her mind and bring her boundless pleasure from just the smallest word or gesture. Jessie had cast her web, and now Louise was tangled in it forever. It was a web she fell into purposefully and completely.

She felt like a ghost that was visiting Jessie at night and snatching a chance at life again. The foreboding woods were dark, but the full moon was shining down a path that would lead to the future. She was drawn to that future and the possibility of a new life and a lasting love. She thought back to the life she once had and realized why she was a ghost—still here. She had unfinished business, unfinished business with her.

"Hey, Jess! Come out here!" Louise called while standing over the group of pumpkins and candles. She watched Jessie walk toward her and had the overpowering urge to surround her with love, to reassure her and comfort her.

Giving up life was hard and painful, but being reborn was so fantastic. That was what she was hoping for, dreaming of, looking for—being reborn into a new life. A life filled with passion, desire, and love. Would she join her in this rebirth or will she remain in that old, steady, reliable state that is really closer to limbo than actual life? The journey had only just begun, and it was going to be long and hard. The future was an unknown path, a risk, and full of uncertainty. But that risk at life was one that she would gladly take for her. No matter the cost to her heart, to her ultimate happiness, or to her very soul. She lingered and watched. She waited with the patience of a ghost that was out of time and place. She waited for her chance. Her chance at life. With her.

It was time to tell Jessie everything.

"Okay. I'm here," declared Jessie as she saw Louise gather candles for the pumpkins. "You're putting candles in now? Shouldn't you wait until it gets dark? It's only ten thirty in the morning."

Louise looked up at Jessie and smiled. The antique pendant hanging around her neck glinted in the sun and glowed with a soft iridescent rainbow. *She is so beautiful,* she thought. "Yes, the candles have to go in now, and they all have to be lit, too." She smiled at Jessie and saw that she was about to object. "All will be explained," she added dramatically before Jessie could speak. "Come with me." Louise handed the candles to Jessie and then picked a pumpkin and led her to the next marked spot. She placed the pumpkin on the ground and looked up at Jessie. "Okay, we'll start here. Put one of the candles inside."

Jessie placed the candle inside the pumpkin and looked at Louise. "Okay, one down. Let's get this done."

"Hold on. We have to light them. We have to light them and say a little spell."

"Oh, my god, Lou. A spell? You're too much!" Jessie laughed. "You really are into this Halloween stuff, aren't you?"

Louise looked at her seriously and took a deep breath. "Jess, this is serious stuff. You remember when we met?"

"Yes. We met November first. Our one-year anniversary is tomorrow. I remember."

"Right, and remember how you said you thought you knew me even though we'd only just met?"

Jessie hesitated. "Yes."

"Well, that's because you did know me. I mean," she hesitated, "Jess, just help me light the candles and say the spell, and then I'll explain everything."

Jessie rolled her eyes. "You're trying to creep me out and scare me, aren't you? Well, it won't work. I'll humor you, but please, Lou, I hate being tricked and scared. Please, don't do that to me, okay?"

"Jess, that's not what I'm doing, I swear. Come on."

"Okay, tell me what to say."

"Right. As you light the candle, we both say together, 'Come power to protect, to fight, and to unite.'"

"That's it?"

Louise nodded and shrugged her shoulders. "That's it. It's been condensed over the years. It used to take about ten minutes per pumpkin, but I finally narrowed it down to the most direct words. It seems that the less you have to focus on a bunch of unnecessary words, the stronger the spell."

Jessie rolled her eyes, again. "Well, I guess that makes sense." A bit of jealousy crept into Jessie's voice. "So you've done this with all your girlfriends?"

Louise looked at Jessie but did not smile. "No, I've only ever done this with you."

Chapter 3

THE PUMPKINS WERE in place around the house, and the candles had been lit with the spell said over each. In the living room, Jessie was sitting on the couch watching Louise as she sat the un-carved pumpkin near the hearth of the fireplace.

Jessie's anxiety was growing because she was sure Louise was trying to freak her out. She finally gave in and burst out with all the questions that had been running through her mind. "Lou, please. Are you messing with me? I'm telling you, I hate being scared. What did you mean I'm the only one you've ever done this with? I thought you said you've done it before. What are you going to do now? Why didn't you carve that pumpkin?"

Louise sat next to Jessie, took her hands, and then gave her a small kiss to make her stop asking questions.

"Jess, I'm not trying to scare you. I have some things I need to explain to you. You may not believe me at first, though. You never do. But if you listen, and if you love me, things will be okay." She looked into Jessie's eyes and could see the confusion and doubt that she had seen so many times before. "Okay, just listen. Try not to interrupt, but if you have questions, please ask me. Okay?"

Jessie sighed and shifted nervously back on the couch. "Okay, I'm listening. Go ahead."

Louise took a deep breath and began explaining the reason for all she had been doing for this, their most recent, first Halloween night.

"The story of us started a long time ago. We had been seeing each other for almost a year, and we hoped to be married."

"Wait. We're women. A long time ago, we'd have been burned at the stake. As a matter of fact, the possibility still exists!" Jessie laughed, still believing that Louise was trying to scare her with her story.

Louise looked into Jessie's eyes without smiling at her attempt at humor. She knew making light of the situation was Jessie's way of coping with her nervousness, but she couldn't let it distract them from what had to be done tonight.

"Jess, do you believe in reincarnation?" Louise waited for Jessie's answer and saw that Jessie had no real answer. "Well," she continued, "we've both been men and women over all of our many lives. You see, love doesn't care what your gender is. It transcends all of that. So, being a man or a woman, it just doesn't matter if your love is true and real. I know ours is, Jess because I've been spending all of my lives trying to live an entire one with you."

"I still don't understand."

"I know," she said patiently. "You see, the first time I gave you that pendant, you had just said you'd marry me. I wasn't planning to ask you that day. I knew there were a lot of obstacles in our way, and I knew giving you a ring was out of the question back then. So, I had planned to just ask you to always love me, knowing that there was a possibility we could never be together. I wanted to give you something that would remind you forever of our love. But you thought I meant to marry you. When you hugged me and kissed me and said, yes, you'd marry me, I just let you think that's what I meant. I wanted that so badly, and I didn't want to make you unhappy."

"So we didn't get married? What happened?"

"No, we didn't get married. We couldn't. Your father had promised you to someone else, and I didn't have the resources to offer that would allow him to break that promise. I knew the situation was almost impossible, but I just couldn't tell you that right then. Later, your father told you the news about who he intended you to marry. You were so angry with him, me—everyone. You sent me a note asking me to meet you on All Hallows' Eve at midnight. I made excuses and got out of my obligations so that I could meet you. Somehow, you got out of the house, and we met in a little hunting cottage in the woods. You arrived before me, and you were upset and cursed everyone and everything into the night."

Jessie nodded. "Sounds like me. I know I'd be pissed if I thought we were getting married, and something stopped us."

"Well, you were," continued Louise. She could see that Jessie still thought she was just being told a Halloween story and did not believe the story was true. "I know you hate the thought of this, and you may not want to believe me, but that night, like tonight, All Hallows' Eve, is a very powerful night. The power isn't good, but it really isn't bad either. You only hear about the bad because, well, it's usually very bad. That night, somehow, your anger at the situation and the events that happened, along with the power that was there, caused something to happen."

"What? What happened?" Jessie asked as she swallowed a lump in her throat and clutched her hands together.

"Like I said, you were angry. I came to meet you. When I stepped inside, you clung to me and cried. My heart just felt like it was being torn right out of my chest. The pain was so unbearable. I held you as you cried, and I felt a black despair wash over me at the thought of our sorry fate. Then, in an instant, our grief turned into terror."

Jessie's eyes opened wide, and she swallowed back her anxiety as Louise continued calmly.

"You didn't know it, but your maid had followed you. When she saw us together, she thought the worst and went to tell your father. He and your betrothed came storming into the cottage. With great anger and no thought to what he was doing, your betrothed shot me in the heart with his shotgun."

Tears crested over the edge of Jessie's eyes. "Shot you? No wonder the first question you asked me when we first met was whether I was with someone or not."

Louise nodded her head slowly and took Jessie's hand. "Yeah, it's no fun being shot." She cleared her throat and continued. "So, I," she hesitated, "I fell to the floor, mortally wounded. I had just seconds to live." Louise stopped as she could see Jessie was deeply riveted by the story. She wanted to give her time to understand that this was not just a story. It was real. "Jessie, are you okay?"

Jessie nodded slowly, her wide eyes blinking at the question, as she pulled herself back into her surroundings. The thought of Louise on the floor dying sent chills through her body. She looked at Louise, then at the hearth with the pumpkin. "So... so what does it all mean?" She was not sure she really wanted Louise to continue, but her curiosity won out. "Why the pumpkins? What happened next?"

Louise took a deep shuddering breath and continued. "As I lay dying, with the sound of the gunshot still ringing in the air, your scream of anguish tore through the night. In those few seconds, it happened."

"*It?*" Jessie whispered so softly that 'it' could barely be heard.

"Something was in the cabin with us, some great power. I think it had been listening to you, to us. I'm not sure if it was being devilish or trying to help. I remember leaving my body. I knew I was dying because I could still feel the pain from the shot pellets. It felt like each one of them was burning inside me. The power reached into me and pulled my ruined heart from my chest and healed it. But my body was finished once it did that so it shoved my heart into a pumpkin that was outside the cottage. After that, for me, everything just went black."

"You…" she swallowed, "you died?"

"Yes. I died," Louise answered quietly.

"Lou, I don't like this story." Jessie tried to get up, but Louise gently pulled her back to the couch.

"I know you don't. But I have to tell it to you, Jess. There's more. Please, let me finish."

Jessie nervously rubbed her neck and face and took a deep breath. "I… I don't like it, Lou. Because…" she hesitated. "Because it's starting to sound familiar and I'm scared."

"I know. You always are. But you have to listen so we can try to get things right this time."

"This time?"

"Jess, I've…" Louise stopped and shook her head. "No, *we've* been doing this for a very long time. Every time we go through this, I find out something new, but every time I have to remind you. You just can't imagine how frustrating that has been for me." She took Jessie's hands and held them to her chest. "Jess, our love is so strong that we keep finding each other. But I'm worried that we'll go on like this forever. I don't want to be a ghost in your life. I want to be with you for a lifetime. Not just for a few days or a year. I want to find a way to end this. So you have to listen, and we have to try to get this right. Okay?"

Jessie's face was shadowed with worry and confusion. *This whole thing was so crazy,* she thought. "Lou, please. Is this real? Are you telling me the truth?"

"Jess, you know I am. You said yourself that things were sounding familiar. So let me finish, okay?" She watched Jessie as she tried to accept this truth. When she felt that Jessie was ready, she spoke again. "So, I died," she started quietly, "but then, one day, I was back. Everything had changed. I was confused. I knew I had died, so I thought that maybe I was in a kind of heaven or in limbo. After a while, I realized I really was alive and that somehow my memories of us had surfaced in the new person I had become. When I was finally able to accept this, I needed to know if I really died and why I was back. I looked for you and other people I knew, but you were all gone. I was traveling the day the memories came back, and I went into a tavern to buy a pint. When I reached in my pocket for some money, I found your pendant. The one I'd given to you before I died. I didn't know what to think at first. But after a while, I remembered that, just before I got all my memories of us back, I had bought it in a local shop. I was already a stranger in the town that I had died in, and now I found myself somehow in a different time. I went to the local press and looked through all the dusty old papers. But still, I found nothing about you. Finally, I asked the priest if I could look through the old church documents and that's where I found you."

"You found me?"

"Yes, I found everything about you that had been recorded by the church. I found out after I had died, you got married."

"Oh, god! Please don't tell me I married the man who killed you!" Jessie cried in horror.

Louise shook her head and stroked Jessie's arm and shoulder to calm her. "No. No, you married someone else."

"Thank god!" Jessie sighed in relief.

"I think he was a good man. You had five children. You died before him. He and your children dedicated a church pew in your memory." Louise let Jessie digest the facts of her former life for a moment and then continued. "I was so mad with grief that you'd died, Jess. I came back to life only to find out that you were gone. I…" She paused. "I'm almost ashamed to say it, but I just wanted to die again. It hurt so much. So, I went to the high footbridge with every intention of jumping to my death. As I was drinking some courage and working up the nerve to throw myself over, I heard a voice."

"A voice?"

"Yes, it was a woman. She was walking across the footbridge. She came up to me, as bold as can be. She told me I should jump or move along, as the bridge was narrow and she needed through. She said she was too busy to wait for me very long. I was angry that she was so cold and uncaring about the anguish I was going through. I turned to curse her, but as soon as I saw her, I stopped. I just stopped and stared at her."

"Why'd you stop? I'd have told her off, too!" Jessie insisted as a protective feeling for Louise flooded through her.

"I stopped," explained Louise, "because she was," she hesitated, "you. She was you!"

"Me?" Jessie asked as her brow wrinkled with doubt.

"Yes. I was stunned. I called out your name. Evelyn."

"My name was Evelyn?"

"Yes. I called out, 'Evelyn it's me, Lucas.'"

"Oh, my god. Your name was Lucas? What were your parents thinking?"

"Jess, please. I don't know what they were thinking. It was a family name, I think, but never mind about that. When we were on the bridge, and I told you my name. You informed me you had no idea who I was and that I was being too forward. You informed me that your name was not Evelyn. It was Clara, and you asked me to kindly move, so… well, I did. But then I followed you and tried to talk to you. Then I had the brilliant idea of giving you the pendant right then. Of course, you refused it, being a proper lady not in the habit of taking gifts from strange men."

"Of course."

"Yes, well. Eventually, you did accept it."

"Because I loved you?"

Louise smiled. "Yes, you did love me. But, once you accepted it…" she stopped as she remembered the pain. "Well, it started."

"*It* again?"

"Yes, the same *it*. It wasn't as powerful as it could have been, luckily, because it was in the summer and not on Halloween night. But still. I died again."

"Again?'

"Again. But I learned something."

"What?"

"Not to give you the pendant until absolutely necessary."

"So," she lingered over the word. "Tonight is necessary?"

"Yes."

"Why? Why do you give it to me? If you give it to me," realization rushed in on Jessie's mind, "you… you'll die! Oh, Lou!

Take it back! I don't want you to die!" She reached for the pendant and tried to take it off, but Louise stopped her.

"No, Jess. It wouldn't matter. Even if I didn't give it to you, I would only get to spend one Halloween with you. I've tried not to give it to you. Still, something always happens, and I die and lose you again. Sometimes, I don't come back for quite a while, and it gets harder and harder to find you. But over the years, each time I came back, it was easier to remember you, and us."

"Lou, if you die every time," she asked hesitantly, "how is it you remember everything and I don't?"

"I'm not sure. But I've learned over time that I have to tell you everything so that we can work together. So I've been trying to figure out how to stop this once and for all. Either I die and stay dead—or I live a real life with you."

"What have you figured out?"

"Well, once, when you were Victor,"

"Wait," Jessie interrupted. "I was Victor? I was a guy?"

Louise nodded. "Yes, like I said, we've both been men and women."

"Yeah," she frowned, "but Victor? I hate that name."

Louise laughed. "Well, Victor, you were very sexy."

"Well, at least I had that. That's good!" Jessie smirked trying to hold back the unease that was beginning to seep into her mind.

"So, when you were Victor, you remembered something that I think is the key to the whole thing. You told me that you remembered hearing a voice that night. You were crying over me, but the voice sounded like it was right up against your ear. It said, 'Love's blood encased in flesh. You must fight all that come and the one at midnight to reunite. Survive twelve, thirteen and half of fourteen, then the life that was taken shall be restored and gain back its mortal time.'"

"It's a riddle?"

"Yeah. I added that bit of information with what I heard before I died and have been using that information to figure out ways to stop the cycle."

"So, what did you hear?"

"Well, from what I heard, I've figured out the pendant works to reunite us and once you are wearing it, well, it declares that we're ready to fight for our love."

"Fight? Lou! So you just decided to put this on me before you told me what it means? That's just great! Now I have no choice!"

Louise looked at Jessie in surprise, her hurt showing in her eyes. "Jessie. I…" She hesitated. "I'm sorry. I didn't think it was something you'd have to think about. I've never had to ask you before." Louise ran her hands through her hair. "Maybe that's why this has never worked. Maybe I'm supposed to ask you and tell you all of this before I give it to you. But you said you'd love me always, I thought. Oh god, Jessie. I'm sorry. I just wanted you to know I will love you always. Please, when I die tonight—"

"Stop it! Lou! Just stop! You are not going to die tonight! Please, I hate this! If you just wanted to get out of going to the Halloween party tonight, you could just say so. Please, don't say things like that! I just can't stand it! Please!" She pulled her hands from Louise's and headed into the kitchen, running her hands nervously through her hair. Louise sadly watched her walk away. Another year. A lifetime for her—wasted. Who knew when she would come back again and how hard it would be to find Jessie. She would be a ghost again.

Chapter 4

LOOKING OUT THE living room window, Louise could see that all but two of the pumpkins they set up for protection had been destroyed. She worked hard all day and into the evening on not bringing up the subject of her death again to Jessie. Now the sadness inside her was heavy, and she had to break her silence. She knew she would have to tell Jessie about what was coming. Jessie was going to be in so much pain after she was gone, and there was nothing she could do about it.

She wanted to live. She wanted to have this life right now!

Right here.

In this house.

With Jessie.

She covered her face with her hands and tried not to think about what she was about to lose again.

A soft touch on her shoulder made Louise look up. Jessie pulled her hand down and around her, and they held each other for a while.

"Jess."

"Lou, please," Jessie said as she looked into Louise's frowning face. Every time she looked at Louise throughout the day, she knew she had more to say. It hung in the air like a dark cloud. "Don't say you're going to die again. I can't take it. It's not funny."

"I know it's not funny, Jess. I need you to look outside. See the pumpkins?"

Jessie looked out and could see only two were still burning. "What happened? Did they go out? Do you want to go relight them?"

"No. Jess, they can't be re-lit." Louise sighed. "They've been smashed, destroyed. By the *ones*, Jess, the ones we have to fight. I need to at least try. I guess I know now what I've been doing wrong, but I still have to try."

"Lou, you didn't do anything wrong. You were right. You didn't have to ask me to fight for you. I do love you, and I'll always fight for you. You never have to ask that. I'm sorry. I'm just scared, and I don't want you to die and leave me, Lou." She pulled Louise close to her and kissed her forehead. "I love you, always."

"Jess, I'm not trying to scare you. I told you, everything is true."

Jessie led Louise back to the couch and sat her down. "So everything is true?" Louise nodded her head, and Jessie continued. "Why is the pumpkin by the fireplace? What's happening with the ones outside?" She looked down at her pendant and then held it up to look at it closer. "How do you always end up with this if you always give it to me?"

Louise took the warm pendant in her hand, looked at it, and then put it back into Jessie's hand. "I'm not sure how I always end up with it. I guess, eventually, you take it off or you pass away, and it just finds its way to me. At first, I would find it, and all of the memories of us come back, but lately, the memories just come suddenly, and then I start looking for the pendant and you. Usually, finding one of you leads to finding the other."

"Why doesn't it find its way to me?"

Louise shrugged. "Maybe because you don't remember it. I always have to remind you about it and tell you what happened."

"Hmm. I guess. So what about the pumpkins?"

Louise looked at the pumpkin on the hearth and sighed because she knew Jessie was not going to like her answer. "It's for my heart."

Jessie's head snapped up, and she looked at Louise with fright in her eyes. "For your heart? Like the first one?"

"Yes. When I die, I can feel my heart being torn out. Just like I did that night. I feel all the pain that I was feeling because you were suffering. I feel all of the pain from every time you've suffered through this. I'm starting to feel that pain now, Jess. It's terrible."

Jessie pulled Louise to her and held her tight. "Oh, Lou, I'm so sorry."

Louise swallowed and buried her face in Jessie's neck. "My heart goes into the pumpkin, and then everything goes black."

"What happens to the pumpkin after your heart goes inside it?

"I don't know." Louise shrugged. "When I come back, I find a seed either in my pocket or in some odd place after I have the awakening. I've always planted it, and every year I live without finding you, I find a seed from the pumpkin I grow."

"So, this is the one you were growing out in the garden?"

"Yeah," Louise nodded.

"What about the ones outside?"

"I just bought those."

"But, why do you need them?"

Louise leaned back so that she could look at Jessie. "I told you. I've been studying all about the power and learning how to protect us from it for as long as possible so that we have time to talk, and I can remind you of things. I put one pumpkin at every hour of the clock. Every hour they come and try to get through the circle. If they aren't strong, they may get through one an hour. But if they are very strong, sometimes, they can destroy more. Once the protective circle is broken, well, we have to fight them. Then at midnight, the 'One' comes."

"The 'One'?"

"I think it's the demon that did this to us. We have to fight it and keep my heart and the pumpkin safe for the time in the riddle. If we do, then it ends. That's my theory now, anyway. So if I'm right, we make it to midnight. Then to thirteen. Which I think is one minute after midnight. Then to half of fourteen—which is seven, so I'm thinking minutes now. I tried seconds last time and, well, it didn't work."

"So, you're pretty sure about this?"

"Yes, as sure as I can be. The whole thing is a guessing game, and I have one shot each time. If I'm wrong, I have to start from the beginning again." Louise leaned back into the couch in frustration.

"Lou, what about the fighting? I'm not sure I know how."

"You know how, Jess. It's just a matter of strength… here…" She put her hand to Jessie's heart. "And here." She put her finger on Jessie's temple. "You have a lot of strength in both of those places."

"Do I? How do you know?"

"Because, Jess, you've done this before, and we almost made it through. You've never doubted our love, and you love me completely. It's the same for me."

"You love me completely?"

"Completely, unconditionally, with all of me. Always."

Jessie was overcome with love for Louise and wrapped her arms around her. They both felt the power of their love for each other coursing through their bodies. A tear ran slowly down Jessie's cheek as she thought about what life would be like without Louise.

The air was thickening around them, and Louise knew the power would be there soon. Slowly, she pulled away from Jessie's kisses and touches. "Jess, it's almost time."

"I love you, Lou," Jessie breathed out heavily through her kisses. "I love you, and I want you with me always."

Louise could feel her heart pounding in her chest at Jessie's words. "I'm always with you, Jess. Always. Don't ever doubt that."

"I won't. Don't leave me, Lou. Please."

Louise looked desperately into Jessie's eyes. "I'll never leave you, Jess. I told you—I'll always be with you. My love is forever. I'll never stop fighting for you."

"Never?"

"Never. Now, let's get ready. We have to fight. It's coming."

Louise cleared a space on the floor. She made a circle with some chemicals from the little jars she bought earlier. When she was finished, they sat across from each other in the circle with the pumpkin between them. They held hands across it and looked deeply into each other's eyes. "So, is any of this becoming more familiar?"

Tears ran thickly down Jessie's cheeks. "Yes. I remember this. I remember a lot of things. I was just afraid to tell you, to say it out loud."

"I know it's hard, but remember, you can do this." Louise squeezed Jessie's hands. They closed their eyes and waited for the power to surround them.

Jessie took comfort in the warmth of Louise's hands. She felt like they had been waiting an eternity. *We really have*, she thought. This had to work. This could not go on forever, could it? She could not lose Lou. She was her heart. The reason she breathed.

A sharp pain tore through her head, and she gasped. She remembered the pain now. She remembered all the tears she had shed. The lives she had led. She remembered the feeling of being alone, even when she had someone by her side. Knowing that the one she really loved, her love, was gone. But she had to go on living, so she had to forget that love. She had to find happiness somehow during the long wait or suffer more and waste away. She had children and pets and friends, husbands and wives. She did love them all, but not with this love. The love that she was feeling in this moment was for only one person—her true and perfect love.

Jessie opened her eyes and looked at Louise. She could see the struggle she was having and knew more was to come her way. A prickling sensation crawled across her skin as some of the invisible power brushed past her. She closed her eyes again and thought only of her love for Louise.

Soon, the couple was surrounded by a wall of power that beat against the shield of love that they had built. But they took the pain and the fear that was set against them. They were clinging to each other over the pumpkin—protecting it in case it must store Louise's heart. They cried out as the power entered their minds and hearts and tormented them. But their love was strong.

Finally, they could feel the power weaken. It ran out of time. They had done it again, now they just had to stay calm and wait. Eight more minutes, then they could leave the circle. They watched the clock and held each other tight. Jessie's anxiety was building. She could not lose Lou. She could not. She could not die. The second hand swept by and another minute passed. *This had to work,* she thought.

Slowly, Louise began to stand. She helped Jessie up, and they watched the final second tick by. It was time. Jessie held Louise back. "Lou, I—"

"It's okay. I have to cross the circle. It's the only way we'll know if I'm right. It's the only way we can start living our whole life together again."

Louise stepped across the circle. She turned and smiled at Jessie.

Jessie watched as Louise fell to the floor. "No!" screamed Jessie. "No!" she cried as she tried to catch Louise as she fell. She was pulled down by the dead weight of Louise's body, and she fell on top of her. "Lou! Lou! No! Don't die!" She looked into Louise's eyes and could see the pain that was there inside her.

Through the crushing pain in her heart, Louise breathed out to speak. She told Jessie it was okay to give her all of her pain so that she could forget. "We'll always be together, Jess. We'll just be different people. I love you, always."

Jessie watched the spark die in Louise's eyes, and she screamed out her pain and anguish into the night.

Chapter 5

THE GALLERY TURNOUT seemed to be a success and, it seemed, the caterer had done an even better job than expected. The hors d'oeuvres were fresh, the champagne glasses full, and there was a smile on everyone's face, including the face of one Rowan Cortman, the orchestrator of the soirée. Rowan had just finished speaking with some new clients and directed them to a piece she was sure they would purchase when she felt a light tap on her shoulder. She turned with a smile and immediately recognized an employee of one of her new clients.

"Eric, isn't it? How are you?"

"I'm fine," he said as he looked at his date with pride and introduced her. "Rowan Cortman, this is—"

"Jessie?" Rowan blurted before she could stop herself.

"No," he laughed, "this is Molly Gentry. Molly Gentry, this is Rowan Cortman," declared Eric.

"How do you do?" asked Ms. Gentry politely.

Out of pure instinct, Rowan answered automatically and offered her hand. "Fine, thank you." She could not help but stare at the antique pendant around the woman's neck as they shook hands for the first time. She had found her again.

Chapter 6

ROWAN PACED HER office with apprehension as she waited for her visitor to make the short trip from the reception area to her office. She had been so stunned last night by the unexpected appearance of Jessie—no, Molly. The night seemed to go by so quickly, and though she tried, she could not get any real time alone to talk with her. She was even more stunned that the pendant was hanging around her beautiful neck.

This was definitely a turn of events.

As sheer luck would have it, Eric's company bought a painting, and Ms. Gentry was on her way in to pick it up now.

What does it mean, Rowan wondered, *that she already had the pendant?*

So many questions and fears were running through her mind. She thought last night something would happen, and she would die again. Molly had the pendant, she was in a relationship with someone, and she seemed to not have any feelings for Rowan at all. Rowan laughed to herself. Molly didn't even know her, so why would she have feelings for her?

Maybe it would all just end before it even started, she thought.

Maybe it will happen today. Death. As Jessie—she shook her head, no—as Molly walked into the office or maybe later tonight. She was surprised it hadn't happened already. *How much time did she have to try to explain things? Would there be enough? Would Molly remember and know her when she heard their story?*

All of those thoughts and questions tumbled through her mind as she waited. Rowan's anxiety was causing her to sweat and her head to throb. She heard Molly's footsteps as she approached the office. She swallowed back her rising fear, wiped her moist hands on her jeans, and prepared herself for the worst. Death. Again.

———————————

MOLLY MADE HER way down the hallway of beautiful artwork and wondered what it must be like to work and to live around such beauty and energy. It almost overwhelmed her senses with color, images, and power. She felt her emotions lift and fall as she passed each incredible piece of art. She saw the door to the gallery owner's office and peeked inside.

How the hell does someone turn out that beautiful? Molly thought as she watched Rowan shift papers on her desk.

At the party last night, as they shook hands for the first time, she had this unnerving feeling come over her. She could feel the warmth and strength of Rowan's hands, and it seemed like such a familiar touch. She could see the way the light shone in her eyes as she smiled, and it took Molly's breath away. Molly did not want to let go of her hand.

The feeling was so unexpected and strange. For a while, it actually made her feel very uncomfortable, so she did her best to keep her distance from the charismatic woman. Of course, she realized she was being silly. She could see that everyone seemed to be drawn to her charming personality. She didn't know why, but she found it hard to not look for her in the crowd and to keep herself focused on the party.

Molly knocked lightly on the door and was rewarded with an absolutely glowing smile as Rowan stood to greet her.

"Come in," said Rowan in her silky voice. She reached into her desk drawer and pulled out an envelope, then smoothly walked around her desk. "I think this is yours," she said as she flashed her breathtaking smile. "I really appreciate you coming to pick up the piece."

Molly blushed at the memory of that embarrassing moment when Rowan described the piece of art with a sensual passion that made her so warm, she had to excuse herself from the room.

"Thank you so much," she said as Rowan placed the envelope with the gallery bill gently in her hand. "It's an amazing piece." She felt the heat of her blush and looked up to find herself staring into the most beautiful liquid brown eyes she had ever seen.

Moments passed as the two women looked into each other's eyes. Rowan was entranced as she always had been each time she found her.

This time, her name was Molly. She had light blonde hair and hazel eyes. Rowan felt like she already knew how it would feel to hold her lithe body close and feel her silky skin. It would be the same familiar and wonderful feeling it was with all of the others Molly had been in her past lives. Lost in the thoughts of the past, and pulled by the love she knew completely, Rowan leaned into Molly and gently kissed her on the lips. She tasted the love she had been seeking for so long.

As Molly suddenly pulled away, Rowan could see the uncertainty and confusion on her face. She realized she made a mistake and that she let her emotions and desire to be with her take over.

"I'm so sorry," she whispered. "I don't know what came over me. You just looked so beautiful and, at that moment, I had to kiss you."

Molly looked at her hands and played nervously with the pendant hanging from her neck. "It," she hesitated, "it's okay. I've never had anything like that happen to me. I guess I'm just not very with it."

"With it?" Rowan asked curiously.

"Yeah, the whole 'kiss anyone you feel like' thing. I guess it's just how I was raised. I'm not from around here," she tried to explain hesitantly.

Rowan laughed and shook her head when she saw that Molly was trying not to lose her cool. "You think I just go around kissing anyone I feel like?"

Molly looked at Rowan's amused smile and became even more uncomfortable. She was not sure if Rowan was laughing at her or the situation. "I, umm, no, I guess not," she stammered.

Rowan watched Molly's hands as she began toying with the pendant nervously again. "That's a beautiful pendant. It looks very old. Did you get it from a family member?"

Molly, looking at the pendant so she didn't have to look at Rowan, realized the conversation had taken a new route. "No. No, actually, I found it," she started but was interrupted by the intercom on Rowan's desk.

The voice of Rowan's assistant, Kevin, came through the speaker. "Ms. Cortman, your two o'clock is here." Rowan reached over the desk and pushed the intercom button.

"Thank you, Kevin. I'll be ready shortly. Please have them wait for me in the conference room. Oh, and Kevin, Ms. Gentry will be down shortly. Please have one of the loaders help her with the piece she's picking up." She nodded as Kevin acknowledged her and then turned back to Molly and offered her hand again. "I'd really like to hear about how you found your pendant. It's a marvelous piece of jewelry. The craftsmanship is exquisite. Would you like to have dinner tonight?"

Molly was surprised at the sudden dinner invitation. Because of the kiss and the intense feelings she'd just experienced, she wasn't sure how to answer.

She noticed she had taken Rowan's hand and hadn't let go yet. She tried not to show her confusion and fear as she pulled her hand away and blurted out her answer. "I—I have a boyfriend, Eric. You remember him?"

"Of course, I remember him. He volunteered your services today," she said as she smiled and looked into Molly's eyes.

Molly swallowed visibly as she took in Rowan's spine melting smile that was directed her way.

"Yeah," she said quietly, "anything to impress the boss." She nervously looked away from Rowan's eyes. "I'll have to check with him. I—I'm not sure if we have plans."

Rowan nodded her head in understanding. "Well, here's my card," she said as she reached for one from her desk and began to write on the back. "I'm giving you my private number. If you change your mind, just call me. I'll be at Valoria's in West Hollywood by seven tonight." She handed Molly the card as they made their way out of the office. "Like I said, I'd love to hear all about your pendant, so call me anytime."

Molly looked at the card with Rowan's perfect handwriting on the back then slipped it into her back pocket.

"Sure, I'll let you know." She gave a slight wave as she turned and headed the opposite direction from Rowan.

She looked back and watched as Rowan turned and walked down the hallway. Molly didn't take her eyes off Rowan's perfect form until she disappeared into the conference room.

She let out the breath she had been holding.

"Wow."

Chapter 7

MOLLY MADE HER way through the crowded restaurant wondering just what exactly she was doing there. She had no intention of calling the gallery owner, let alone agreeing to have dinner tonight. But when she told Eric about the invitation and Ms. Cortman's interest in her pendant—leaving out the kiss, of course—he was adamant that she go.

She knew why he wanted her to go. She just didn't know why she let him convince her. He wanted the bragging rights that came with having the private number of the most prestigious and beautiful Ms. Cortman in his contact circle. He wanted to use the opportunity as a stepping-stone to richer clients and more money for himself.

Apparently, his girlfriend was now in some sort of select club with a person whom Eric claimed was, on top of everything else, the sexiest woman ever. Molly was not sure if she even wanted to be in that club, but she was here now.

"Sexiest woman ever?" Molly mumbled under her breath while looking even more uneasy as she searched the crowd for the president of that select club.

"Ms. Gentry?" asked a thick Italian-accented voice.

Molly turned and found herself in the presence of a smiling woman who exuded pure sexuality. She was surprised because she had no idea who the woman was, but she hesitantly answered. "Yes, I'm Molly Gentry."

The woman looked at Molly, sized her up, and nodded her head in apparent approval. "I am Valoria. Rowan. Ms. Cortman is waiting for you. Follow me. I will take you to her."

Molly followed Valoria through the restaurant. She watched as Valoria stopped and made comments to guests and gave instructions to waiters as they made their progress toward the back. They came to a semi-private alcove where Molly realized the woman standing to greet her was Ms. Cortman. She was transformed, stunning, and looked even more beautiful and exotic in her evening outfit and with her dark hair stylishly coifed. Molly blushed when she realized she was staring.

Rowan smiled and signaled Molly to take a seat. "I'm so glad you decided to come."

"Thank you for inviting me," Molly replied as she took her seat.

"I'll bring you some wine," offered Valoria. "The Italian, of course. Red, I think," she mused as she headed toward the bar.

Molly watched her leave and then turned back to Rowan. "Is she the owner?"

"Yes, she and her partner own Valoria's. It's a café during the day and a dinner club in the evenings."

"Oh," said Molly as she looked around noticing that there were mostly women in the club. "I'm not gay," she blurted and then nervously bit her lip.

Rowan laughed and patted her hand across the table. "That's okay. You don't have to be gay to have dinner here." She watched Molly and could see just how uncomfortable she was as she began toying with her pendant. "Molly, if you're uncomfortable, we can go somewhere else."

"Oh, no. No, it's fine, really." She looked up at Rowan and could not stop herself from blushing again.

"Okay," said Rowan as she picked up her menu. "Valoria is coming with our wine. Why don't we see what we'd like to eat?"

Rowan directed the dinner conversation to topics that she hoped would help Molly feel less nervous. They talked about Molly's career in the film industry that she hoped to build and about her boyfriend, Eric, and his job. They talked about her family, what was left of it anyway, who lived in the Midwest, and also about her childhood.

Rowan listened to her every word as if trying to memorize them. She wanted to know all about this new person that her love had become. "It sounds like you've had a very happy life," Rowan commented. "Tell me about the pendant that has brought us together…" she paused, "for dinner this evening," she said quickly catching herself as she saw Molly's eyes widen.

Molly looked into her glass, took a sip of her rich, sweet wine, and nodded her head. "Sure. Well, let's see," she began. She looked up and wrinkled her brow slightly as she remembered. "I was about fourteen, I think."

"Fourteen?" Rowan asked, very surprised at this information. She was sure it had to have been a recent find. She never knew when the pendant would show up in her life, but she knew it usually wasn't long after finding it that she found her.

Molly nodded and pursed her lips. "Yes, I was fourteen. I was staying with my cousins just outside New York for the summer when their elderly neighbor passed away. She had so much stuff in her house that the family decided to have a big sale to get rid of everything that no one wanted. Apparently, a lot of the stuff belonged to a great aunt and was passed to her niece and her husband who inherited the house when she died. When they both died, the family decided to sell it and everything inside."

"I used to live in New York. It's a small world," Rowan added with a smile.

"I guess," shrugged Molly. "Anyway, I went to the sale. There were boxes and old trunks just full of treasures. But one old trunk caught my eye, and I had to discover what was inside. I opened it, and it was full of old news clipping albums, letters, and some old books."

"Books? I thought you were looking for treasure." Rowan laughed.

"I was. Books were treasures to me and cookbooks were treasures to my grandma. So, there were some old cookbooks, a few hardback books, and books that looked like they were handwritten. I thought they were full of old recipes that someone had written down, and I wanted them for my grandma. She loved getting new recipes." Molly smiled as she remembered her grandmother with fondness. "I loaded the chest in my little cousins' wagon and asked the lady what she wanted for the trunk full of cookbooks. The lady dug through the trunk and said she wanted ten dollars for the lot."

"Wow. That was a lot for a fourteen-year-old."

Molly nodded. "I was so disappointed because I knew I didn't have that much money. So, I pulled out my change purse and started counting out what I had onto the table hoping somehow the money I knew wasn't there would magically appear." Molly smiled to herself as she remembered the dreams and fantasies of her fourteen-year-old self. "Of course, it didn't magically appear. I had exactly five dollars and forty-three cents." Molly sighed at the memory. "I was so disheartened. I was about to ask the lady if she'd hold the trunk for me so I could go try and find more money."

"Ah, the old beg, steal, borrow, and search through the couch cushions. I've been there." Rowan laughed.

"Exactly," Molly confirmed. "But then my little cousin Teddy showed up and started screaming and throwing a fit because I had his wagon. He was trying to pull it away while screaming it was his, and I was trying to tell him to wait because I needed it. He just got louder and louder, and people were watching us struggle against each other over the wagon. Finally, the lady had enough. My money was still on the table, and she told me to take the trunk, the wagon, and the brat away!" Molly laughed at the situation she was describing. "I was so happy, I let go of the wagon and hugged the lady. Teddy fell over and started crying instead of yelling. I looked at Teddy, and I just wanted to kiss him." Molly blushed and held in her mirth. "I did kiss him!" She laughed spiritedly. "He jumped up after I kissed him and ran home screaming, 'Mom, Mom, help! Molly kissed me! I'm gonna die! I'm gonna die!' At that moment, I didn't care about anything but my new trunk full of books. I grabbed the handle to the wagon and skipped all the way home."

"Thank god for annoying little cousins!" Rowan contributed as she laughed. Molly's laughter mixed with Rowan's, and after a while, they both regained their composure. "So," she hesitated, "so when did you find the pendant? I'm assuming it was in the trunk." Rowan's heart fluttered in her chest at the sight of the sparkle in Molly's eyes.

Molly nodded as she put her wine glass back on the table. "It was. But I didn't find it until a couple of days later. It was raining out, and we were stuck inside so I decided to go through the trunk. I had pulled almost everything out and sorted things into two piles. One pile for 'interesting' and the other was the 'looks like junk' pile." Molly looked up, as Rowan chuckled at her teenage sorting technique, and smiled. "I pulled out this…" Molly grimaced, "package, I guess. It was wrapped in plain paper and tied with string to keep it together. I was so excited! It was like an early Christmas present. I unwrapped it and found some journals and a box. Of course, I set the journals aside and went straight for the box!"

"Of course, you did," said Rowan. "What kid wouldn't?"

"Right!" Molly laughed. "Well, inside the box were a stack of love letters tied with a silk ribbon and a small tooled leather box." Molly smiled at Rowan. "I went for the box again! I opened it, and there it was. The most beautiful thing I'd ever seen. The pendant was so beautiful, I started feeling guilty because I bought everything in the trunk for five dollars and forty-three cents!"

"You definitely got a bargain," said Rowan and slowly sipped her wine. "What'd you do?"

"I took it downstairs and showed it to my aunt and uncle. They looked at it and told me that I should just keep it because it was only a gaudy and flimsy piece of costume jewelry." Molly watched Rowan as she said nothing but raised her eyebrows slightly. "Well, that made me happy. I didn't care that it was worthless. I thought it was beautiful."

"It is beautiful," agreed Rowan.

Molly looked down at the pendant. "I remember I ran back upstairs and stood in front of my mirror and put it on. It's strange how a silly piece of cheap jewelry can make you feel so good. It still does."

Rowan looked at Molly and frowned. She hesitated for a moment and sighed. "Molly," she said with confidence, "I'm pretty sure your aunt and uncle were wrong about that pendant."

"What do you mean?" asked Molly a bit confused.

"Well, how closely have you looked at that pendant?"

"What?"

"Did you happen to notice the writing on it?"

Molly looked closely at the pendant and turned it over in her hands. "Writing?"

"Yes, on the lower edge there should be a maker's mark—a signature." Rowan was tempted to take the pendant and show Molly the signature, but she was afraid of what may happen if she touched it now. Instead, she handed Molly her jewelers' glass to look through. "Here. Look through this."

Molly held the jeweler's glass over the back of the pendant and squinted at the tiny marking that was worn and darkened from age. "It looks like," she looked closer, "l-a-l-i-q-u-e. Lalique." She looked up at Rowan with wide eyes. "Oh, my fuck," she said in surprise. "Lalique! Fuck!"

"Yes," Rowan smiled amused at her response.

"I… oh, my god. I've been wearing this around almost everywhere since I was fourteen! But it's so light," she said as she looked at it again. "Is it some kind of fake metal or maybe a copy?"

Rowan laughed. "I can guarantee you that pendant is made of pure silver and not a copy. It's an Art Nouveau piece from the late 1880s. It is one of the early pieces made by René Lalique. They weren't really concerned with the weight of the silver back then as much as the beauty of the design. A lot of people make mistakes, like your aunt and uncle, because they think silver and gemstones should look a certain way." Rowan took a sip of her wine to let Molly absorb the information. "The stone is a moonstone. It gets its name because of the way it glows and looks different whenever it changes position. Now this is just a small one, mind you, but it's still very nice and, though it looks dark in this light, it's really very clear with a slight blue color."

"Moonstone," Molly mumbled as she looked closely at the pendant.

"That's right. If you get the pendant cleaned it'll get rid of the grime, and you'll see the silver and the color of the stone better." Rowan hesitated for a moment and watched Molly admire her pendant. "The moonstone is known as the stone of lovers. It's supposed to bring forth feelings of tenderness," she hesitated, "and to protect true love."

Molly looked up quickly at Rowan. "Protect true love?" She watched as Rowan slowly nodded her head. "It makes sense now, kind of."

"Makes sense?"

"The letters and the journals—sort of."

"Letters? Journals?"

"Yes, remember I told you there were letters and journals wrapped with the pendant?"

"I remember."

Molly took a breath getting very excited. "I remember that was the weekend my aunt and uncle were planning to take us to the Met because they had a special art exhibit for children, and they wanted all of us to do at least one constructive thing during the summer. But Teddy got an earache, and we had to stay home."

"You were planning to go to the Met?" Rowan asked, and frowned slightly. "How old are you?"

Confused Molly answered, "I'm twenty-six, why?"

"That means when you were fourteen I was nineteen."

"So?"

"It was my first year in college, and for the summer, I volunteered at the Met. Do you realize that if you'd gone, we'd have met back then? I remember the exhibit because I worked as an assistant to the curator that put it together. I even got to do some of the public tours."

"That is so crazy! It's like we just missed each other, and all because of my bratty cousin Teddy." They sat in silence pondering that thought.

After a while, Molly broke the silence as she looked at her watch. She had begun to feel self-conscious because she had rambled on about the day she found the pendant. "Oh, it's getting late. I really should start heading home."

Rowan looked at Molly, still caught up in the thought that they actually could have met years ago, and she already had the pendant back then. *What could it mean?* Her thoughts were interrupted by Molly as she started to stand up. "Oh, right. I guess it is getting late. I'll walk you to your car."

"Thank you. I had a wonderful evening," Molly said hesitantly. For some reason, she had a strong feeling she wanted to stay close to this woman. "Dinner was wonderful."

"You're very welcome," Rowan replied. "Maybe we can do this again sometime."

"Sure." Molly nodded. "Definitely."

Chapter 8

ROWAN COULD NOT stop thinking about Molly and the pendant. She felt like she was losing control. Molly actually had the pendant—and she had it for years. *How was that possible*, she asked herself. It was astounding they had not met when they were much younger when Molly first found the pendant. Nothing was happening as it had in the past—nothing except the strong pull she had toward Molly and the need to be close to her.

Rowan was in her bed alone, and she wanted Jessie—no, Molly there with her. She wanted to be holding her. Rowan closed her eyes, and she saw Jessie's face morph into Molly's face in her mind.

Memories resurfaced, and she could feel that familiar longing inside her again. She sighed as Molly ran her hands over her body tenderly and as they kissed deeply, sweetly. Rowan could feel Molly's kisses on her face and neck and could hear her whisper and sigh in her ear that she wanted her and needed her.

Molly ran her hands under Rowan's shirt and moved them over her warm body making her temperature rise and her breathing heavy. Molly knew that Rowan couldn't resist her touch, and she pulled off Rowan's shirt then pressed her body against her.

She pushed Rowan back and lightly ran her fingers over Rowan's ribs and stomach as she made her way down Rowan's body to the button and zipper of her jeans. She tugged Rowan's jeans and pulled her hips up, sliding the jeans off, and dropping them on the floor. She crawled back up Rowan's body and straddled her. She looked down on Rowan with her beautiful hazel eyes and slowly, with a sexy, sensuous smile, started to take her own shirt off and over her head.

Rowan took hold of Molly's hips and moved her hands over her, making her way to Molly's snap and zipper. Molly leaned over Rowan and put her hands on either side of her head and kissed her as Rowan slid her jeans down over her hips.

Molly did not let Rowan get them half way down before she moved up so that her breasts were over Rowan's face, and she lowered herself so that Rowan's tongue could reach her nipple and then she lowered herself into Rowan's mouth.

As Rowan sucked gently on Molly's breast, she moaned while Rowan's hands worked on getting Molly's jeans the rest of the way off.

Molly lifted herself off Rowan and kicked the jeans to the floor and then moved back onto her. She pressed herself against Rowan, and she could feel how hot and wet Molly was against her stomach. Molly pressed herself down and moved her center rhythmically against Rowan and then leaned down to whisper in her ear, "You want me?"

Rowan's body started to shake, and her head spun. She licked her lips and swallowed back down her heart that had jumped out of her chest at the sound of Molly's sensual voice in her ear. She tried to regain some control, but it was useless. She struggled to speak through the desire Molly had caused in her. "I want you. God, I love you!" Rowan said out loud but woke herself up, still reaching for Molly and realizing that it was only a dream. She threw herself back onto her pillows. "Fuck!"

Rowan put her arm over her eyes and thought about her dinner with Molly. *She had that pendant since she was fourteen,* she thought. *How could that be? This was definitely new.*

She was up against a lot this time—the mystery of the pendant and the boyfriend, not to mention the fact that Molly was very uncomfortable about the thought of being in a relationship with another woman.

She had been through the same-sex relationship problem before. With Jessie and again when they were Roger and Mark. Mark just could not get past how he had been raised and the guilt he felt whenever they were together.

After he as Roger had died on Halloween, Mark's life went downhill because he had felt even more guilt, and it ate him up inside. Mark turned to drugs and alcohol and died when he 'fell' off a bridge one night, leaving a wife and two kids behind. *God,* Rowan thought, *I hope it doesn't happen like that again.* Finding out the person she loved so deeply had suffered so badly made her heart ache terribly. She wanted to end both of their sufferings.

They had to get things right this time.

Chapter 9

SOFT ROMANTIC MUSIC filled the room, and the sweet smell of roses from the scented candle on the coffee table filled the air. Molly moaned as she stretched her arms above her head and arched her back off the couch.

She was surrounded by love in the form of letters written long ago. A smile made its way to her face as she realized the letters still made her feel the way she did when she first read them at fourteen. With every word she read, she could feel the power of the intense love the writer had for their lover. She could see everything in her mind like it was her own moment, her own memory.

Sitting up on the couch, Molly folded the letter carefully and put it back in its envelope. As she reached toward the stack of unread letters for another to read, she heard the door to her apartment open and the sound of Eric entering.

"Hey, babe," she called. "I'm in here."

Eric made his way into the living room and was met with the sight of Molly surrounded by piles of old books and papers that had apparently come from the old trunk that was sitting in the middle of the area rug. He looked around in confusion. "What are you doing?"

Molly smiled up at him. "I've decided to start a new project."

"A new project?" Eric asked and gave Molly a small kiss.

Molly motioned to the papers surrounding her. "I'm going to transcribe and turn all of these love letters and journals into a screenplay based on the lives of the people in them," she explained excitedly.

"A screenplay? Molly…" Eric shook his head in disbelief. "You can't write a screenplay. I mean, you've never written one before. Besides, it's just a waste of time."

"What? A waste of time? I don't think it is." Molly looked at Eric in disbelief. "Eric, I do have a degree in literature and film studies, and I have read hundreds of screenplays. I know I've never written one before, but I'm smart enough to know where to go if I need help."

"Molly, you know how many screenplays get chucked into the bin. I'm telling you, you'll just be wasting your time. Besides, it takes ages to write one sometimes, and you'll be busy doing other things."

"I don't know what other things you're talking about," said Molly dispirited. "Rowan thought it was a great idea."

"Rowan? Rowan? Oh, yes, your good friend Rowan," Eric retorted sarcastically. "Did you know she had two parties last month, and we didn't get invited to either? Great friend she is!"

"What's wrong with you tonight?"

"What's wrong with me?" he exclaimed as he paced in agitation. "Well, let's see. I come over to pick you up for dinner." He turned and looked angrily at her. "Dinner. You remember—the one we're expected at for my job? I walk in and find you not dressed and buried in a stack of musty old letters. So I can only assume that you forgot about dinner. Oh, and I lost out on a big client today, a really big client, and now you tell me that your so-called friend Rowan Cortman thinks wasting your time on a fucking screenplay is a 'great' idea! Is that enough for you?"

"She is my friend, Eric," Molly said trying to stay calm as she put away the books and papers. "She's not a stepping stone for your greed!"

"It's called networking, Molly! Networking! It's how things get done, and money is made!"

"Those parties were for charity! She invited people who would support the charity she was sponsoring, not to network with you!"

Eric looked at her suspiciously. "So, she invited us? She invited us, and you turned down the invitation! Great, Molly!"

"No, she didn't invite us. We weren't on the invitation list of people who would possibly contribute!"

"Well, how does she know I can't contribute?"

"Oh, my god! So, you're telling me that you would have actually gone to a party for the opening of a show called 'Contemporary Art of the Modern Black Woman in Crisis'? And you would have paid a thousand dollars a plate for the dinner? Then, on top of that, you would have made a substantial contribution to the foundation Rowan arranged the party for?" She looked at Eric angrily and continued to make her point. "Oh, and the other one. I'm sure it was right up your ally! It was called 'Children in Mourning - Their Creations and Memories' where she was helping raise money for a charity that helps children who have lost a parent. Oh, and the dinner at that one was fifteen hundred dollars a plate and most of the guests were expected to make a ten thousand dollar contribution. Eric, you couldn't afford to go to either one!"

"Hey! I may have been able to get my company to contribute! She didn't even ask if we'd be interested!"

"She didn't have to ask! For your information, she had the owner of your company on her invitation list! She didn't have to invite you!"

"Well, fuck her! You're supposed to be her friend! She could have let us come for free!"

"Eric, you are such an ass! The whole point was to make money for charity—not to start one for you!"

"Fuck you, Molly! You saw her invitation list? Why didn't you say anything to me about it? Then I would have at least known the owner of my company was going!" Eric looked at her fuming. "Are you fucking her?"

"What?" she asked as she was taken aback by the question.

"It's a simple question. You've been spending a lot of time with her, and all you ever talk about is Rowan this and Rowan that! Are you?"

Molly was seething inside at the foundless accusation. She replied angrily through clenched teeth, "Eric, she is my friend."

"She's gay, you know. Well, sometimes. I hear she says she loves a person's soul, not the gender. What a load of crap! I'll bet that line has gotten her laid a lot!"

Molly's anger burst from her. "Get the hell out! Go to your fucking dinner by yourself! Get out!"

"No! You have to go! You made a commitment, and as my girlfriend, you have to honor that commitment!"

"You know what? If you don't get out now, you may just be looking for a new girlfriend. I don't like you much right now. Why are you being such a fuck?" Molly yelled.

"Is that a threat?"

"Take it however you want! You're such a bastard!"

"Well, you're a bitch!" he shot as he turned and walked toward the door. "I may just find a new girlfriend tonight!"

"Fine!"

"Fine!" Eric retorted and slammed the door to make sure he got the last word.

Molly cringed at the sound of the door slamming and sat back on the couch shaking and trying to calm down. Tears began to fall down her cheeks, and she sobbed as all her other emotions kicked in alongside her anger.

"Why does he do things like this?" she asked the empty room. "I hate this. I can't take it!"

She lay down on the couch and curled up in a ball like a child hiding in the night. Soon, her breathing calmed, and her body became weak from holding her muscles tense for so long. She took a deep breath then released, relaxing her muscles.

She hated it when they fought, and he just seemed to be starting more fights lately. She could not believe he had gone so low as to accuse her of sleeping with Rowan. She laughed a bit at the thought.

Besides the fact that she would not cheat on him, and has never cheated, she had not even considered doing anything like that with Rowan. Molly laughed out loud.

"He'd probably love it if I did and would pay to join in, the creep. I'm not a lesbian."

She buried her face in the couch pillow and sighed sadly. *It was a good thing I never told him about that kiss,* she thought. She fell asleep, wondering if things were really over between her and Eric.

Chapter 10

THE SOUND OF the ocean waves crashing onto the deserted beach thundered through the evening air making its way toward Molly. She leaned on her elbows against the rail of the large deck that looked out over the sea. The cool wind played gently with her hair. She could feel the warmth of the wine run through her as she sipped it from her glass. She put her glass on the railing and breathed in the perfect scent of the sea air. She looked up and was amazed at how enormous the moon seemed to be against the night as it glowed a golden hue upon the glistening water.

"Beautiful," whispered Rowan as she joined Molly on the deck.

"Yes, it is." Molly sighed as she looked at Rowan then back out at the sea. "The moon looks so close to us."

Rowan stood silently next to Molly, unsure whether she should tell her that she was not talking about the moon.

Molly looked back at Rowan and smiled. "Thank you for inviting me here."

"You're very welcome," Rowan said as she smiled. "I like coming out here to get away from the city. I'm lucky Valoria is a good friend and lets me use her beach house."

"I'm sorry for venting so much to you about Eric." She sighed and looked into her glass at the rich red color of the wine.

"Don't worry about it." Rowan shrugged. She would listen to anything just to be close to her. "I could see that something was wrong, and I did ask."

"Still," said Molly worried that Rowan was tired of being around her. The wine was causing her to open up and spill everything that was on her mind before she could stop herself.

"Still," answered Rowan wishing they had more than a weekend to spend together.

Molly turned and sat down on the soft lounger. Rowan was so easy for her to talk with. Like a best friend that she had suddenly found again. She took another sip of her wine and looked up at the bright stars. "I don't know what's going on with him. I haven't heard from him all week."

Rowan sat on the lounger next to Molly's chair and set her wine glass on the table. "I do feel a little responsible because we really have been spending a lot of time together."

"It wasn't your fault at all," Molly said as she shook her head, and her vision swam a bit from the effect of the wine. "He would have found some reason to blow up, he always does. Besides, I love spending time with you."

"You do?"

Molly laughed at Rowan's surprise. "Yes, I feel good when we're doing things together, even when we're just talking. Like now."

Rowan could not help but smile as a rush of love for this woman filled her. "Well, I'm here for you anytime."

Molly sighed heavily as she thought about Eric. "He says writing the screenplay is a waste of time."

What? But it's something you're so excited about."

"I know," Molly said sadly.

"Molly, you have to do things in this life that make you happy and that you're excited about doing. Life is so short." Rowan stopped. It was so frustrating to her that people ended up wasting their lives and actually chose to be miserable.

She had seen it happen over and over. She always knew that her life would be short until the curse could be broken. She also knew when she finally had a whole life to live she was not going to waste a moment.

"What I mean to say is, if he really loved you, he'd support you," she said. "He wouldn't tell you that the things you're passionate about are a waste of time."

Molly shrugged and set her glass down on the table next to Rowan's glass. "He says I'll be busy with other things. I'm not sure what that means."

Rowan almost choked on her wine as she laughed. "Other things?" She watched Molly nod and could see she was a bit annoyed and drunk. "Molly, I think he's trying to tell you that he thinks you're going to be his good little wife, and the other things you'll be busy with are taking care of him, the kids, and the house, probably in that order."

"No," Molly disagreed. "We've talked, and he knows I plan on building my career. I told him I don't want to have kids until I'm set in my career, and even after I have a child, I plan to work. I love my career choice, and I want to take it as far as I can. I mean, you make it sound like the dark ages. A woman can have children and a career today."

"I know, I know. But Molly, writing this screenplay goes along with your career choice," Rowan said as she tried not to put Molly on the defensive but still get her point across. "It's just, to me anyway," she hesitated, "I could be wrong, but it sounds like he is saying your career is just something he'll tolerate now, but if you get married, then…" She let the word hang in the air.

"What? You think he'll want me to be a housewife or something?" She watched as Rowan shrugged and looked at her sympathetically. "I don't think he's that old fashioned. Besides, he hasn't even asked me to marry him yet. We're just dating."

"Oh, I see."

"What? What do you see?"

"You're just dating." Rowan took a sip of her wine and loved the light feeling it caused in her. "So, do you love him? If he asks, will you say yes?"

Molly hesitated and was surprised that her answer was not blurting out of her. "I, uh, I do love him. I don't know what I'd say if he asked me, though. I don't think I'm ready for that yet. Things just don't feel right."

"But you love him?" Rowan asked trying to hide her sadness.

"I guess."

"You just said you did."

"Well, there are lots of kinds of love."

"Molly! You know the kind of love I'm talking about. Marriage, a life together, forever love. Do you?"

"I—" she stopped herself for a moment. "This may sound crazy but, I do love him. I just don't know if I'm 'in' love with him. I'm not even sure if I know what being 'in' love means."

Rowan shook her head. "No, that doesn't sound crazy. A lot of people feel that way. But you can't just settle and hope you'll end up happy. You have to find the person you'll be happy with and want to be with for the rest of your life. It's not like buying a cheap car just to get by. You have to be sure."

"No one is ever happy every moment in a relationship. You have to work hard and make it work."

"That's true. But you have to be with someone you'd want to work hard *for*. Someone who you'd move heaven and earth for, and with every backbreaking moment of it, you'd never complain because they mean everything to you. And they should feel the same way."

"Sounds like you're in love." Molly watched as Rowan looked away. "Are you?"

Rowan looked back and straight into Molly's eyes and held her gaze for a moment before answering. "Yes."

Molly broke the gaze and looked down confused. She did not really understand the sudden wave of pain and jealousy that ran through her. "Oh," she whispered quietly. "You know, you've never talked to me about your love life. Is she someone you'd work that hard for?"

"Yes, I've been working very hard."

Molly continued to look at her hands and sighed. "I didn't tell you this before, but Eric accused me of having an affair with you."

"Really?" Rowan replied dryly.

Molly gave Rowan a small smile. "Yeah, he did. He made a big deal to me about you being gay." She hesitated. "Are you? I mean, I know that you know people who are. Who doesn't? And you go to Valoria's and stay here at her place and all but—"

"Does it matter?"

"No," Molly whispered. "It doesn't."

"That's good. I always know the person I love, and it has never mattered to me whether they are a man or a woman. I know our souls are connected, and we are meant to be together."

"How many people have you been in love with?"

Rowan looked at Molly and knew she would be confused by what she would say, but she answered honestly. "Just one." Rowan did not give Molly too much time to think of a reply and changed the subject. "Tell me more about the letters and journals you want to turn into a screenplay. That's much more interesting than me."

Molly looked at Rowan with a lot of confusion. It didn't help that her mind was muddled from the wine. She could see that her friend didn't want to go any further down that path, and so she complied. "Okay. Let's get some more wine first."

———

ROWAN SAT ON the couch and looked at the familiar wooden box Molly had brought over that was sitting on the coffee table. Jessie bought it when they went on a road trip across the countryside and always had it on her dresser. She said it reminded her of the changing colors of the autumn leaves. Rowan carefully and thoughtfully opened the box. She saw the tooled leather jewelry box inside that held the pendant she had given Jessie on their last night together.

Rowan carefully picked up the small box that belonged with the pendant and stroked the soft leather and traced the tooled design as her wine-altered mind filled with memories of another life. She did not have to open the box because she knew the pendant was resting around Molly's neck, but she opened it anyway out of habit. She looked at the black velvet lining that held the impression of the pendant and smiled at the similarity of the empty box to her life.

The box was specially made to hold something very precious, and nothing else really fit perfectly inside, just like her heart. She looked up as Molly brought in a fresh bottle of wine and refilled their glasses. In Molly, she saw the precious soul that fit her heart perfectly.

"Here you are," Molly said as she handed Rowan her glass.

"Thank you," said Rowan.

Molly sat on the couch with Rowan and got comfortable. She took a fortifying sip of wine and got her thoughts together about the story she wanted to write. "Well, let's see. Like I said, it's a tragic love story."

"You didn't say it was a tragic love story," Rowan frowned.

"Oh. Well, it is." She picked up her notes and flipped through them. "The letters were written by a couple, Jessie and Lou. There are a few letters written by Jessie after Lou died, and she also wrote everything in the journals as if she was talking to him.

"Him?"

"Yes, Lou," Molly confirmed. "He died suddenly of a heart attack from what I can tell and she never got over it. She didn't want to get over it. I think she may have gone a little mad."

"Mad?" asked Rowan, concerned about how much Jessie may have suffered.

"She started having delusions that he would come back, and she wrote an elaborate narrative about how they were different people over the years, and they only had until Halloween night to be together.

"The journals that I thought were recipes were the spells that she worked out to try and bring her lover back to her. I know it sounds crazy, but it's really quite romantic. What I'd like to do is transcribe everything to make it easier to read. That way I don't have to keep handling the letters and journals. Then I can put it together as a screenplay for a movie or a mini-series. I think the story is compelling enough for either of those."

"I don't think the story sounds crazy at all. Jessie must have loved Lou very much," Rowan replied sadly as she looked at the stack of love letters on the table.

"She did," Molly said as she looked at her notes again. "Jessie wrote that the curse, not a heart attack, killed Lou. She started out very angry with Lou for not telling her about everything sooner, but then she set aside her grief and created a mission for herself to try and help break the curse." She leaned forward and looked through the stack of letters and handed two of them to Rowan for her to read.

> *Lou,*
>
> *I think I've cried every kind of tear imaginable over losing you. Now I have to pick myself up and live what is the rest of my life without ever looking into your beautiful eyes again.*
>
> *I had one of my epiphanies today while I was reading your love letters for what seems like the thousandth time.*
>
> *I shall give up my grief today.*
>
> *Instead of grieving, I will continue fighting on after your death.*
>
> *I've been thinking a lot about the things you told me on our last night together. It's so hard to think about that night sometimes. I believe I see a pattern that may be the reason the curse has remained unbroken.*
>
> *The reason is, in all of my many lives, I've always moved on, and the circle was broken because of it. Instead of fighting the curse, I let it control me and drown me in grief and pain. I allowed myself to forget again so I could live out my life with the illusion of happiness.*

Today, I have decided to take control and to make it my life's mission to make sure, when my soul is here again, the person I become will know our story even before we meet again.

My hope is that these letters we have poured all of our love into will help my soul know you before it ever meets you.

I will not feel grief now because I know the most important thing is still with me, our love. I know our souls will be reunited, so grieving any more would be a waste of time since we are destined for each other.

Lou, I will do everything in my power to make sure the next time we meet, we will be together for a lifetime.

Yours eternally,

Jess

Lou,

My love, after so many years of researching, and so much trial and error, I believe that I've found another way to make sure my soul can learn our story before we meet again.

Now, at the end of my life, it is time to put it to the test.

I am using the pendant as an anchor for this spell.

My fear is that if it doesn't work, and the pendant is lost to us, I will have made things worse. But I have to try.

I'm hoping my spell will be secondary to whatever the curse did, and it will still find its way to you. But this time, I should already have it and our story in my possession.

I've recorded everything in my journals so that if it fails, I will have records to start with again, as I know I may not remember anything from this life like all the times before.

My request to you, my love, if this letter finds you, is that you write down your memories and add all of our other stories to this one for our future selves.

I know how you suffer when you think I've been unhappy, but my love, you have given my life purpose and meaning, and I can think of no other way I would have wanted to spend it than finding my way back to you.

In these last hours, I am not afraid, because I know that I shall return.

My heart is filled with so much joy at the thought that I will love you again soon.

Yours eternally,

Jess

———————

ROWAN PLACED THE letters down on the table carefully and took another long drink of wine. She found some answers to her questions, but now she had so many more running through her mind. Before she could utter any of her questions, Molly cleared her throat and went on with the story.

"She wrote a lot of notes to herself in the journals about how she thought the reason the curse hadn't been broken before was because the failure was on her end. I think she was feeling a lot of guilt that she had a whole life to live when Lou didn't. Everything is so detailed and organized. I imagine it's the way I would have put things together if I were doing the research. It's strange when I read her journals I get déjà vu sometimes. I guess it's because I read some of them when I was younger."

Rowan looked at Molly as she flipped through her notes wanting so badly to tell her everything now but afraid she would think she was as mad just as she thought Jessie was. The effects of reading the letters from Jessie, having Molly so close to her now, and having to hold in all of her emotions was beginning to overwhelm her.

She leaned forward and put her face in her hands using the tips of her fingers to catch and hide the tears that slowly seeped out of her. She took a deep breath to collect herself then picked up her glass and leaned back on the couch.

"So, do you wear the pendant because you believe what she's saying may be true, that the pendant will find Lou?" she asked without looking at Molly.

Molly blushed as she remembered the dreams of her youth. "I…" she hesitated. "When I was young, I'll admit I was caught up in the romance of the story. I used to pretend I was Jessie and every boy I looked at I would wonder if it was Lou. I'd imagine that he would look me in the eyes and kiss me and…" She stopped.

"And what?" asked Rowan her curiosity made her eyebrows raise.

"Nothing," Molly said quickly and took a sip of wine thinking of the kiss that she shared with her.

Rowan watched Molly as she nervously ran her fingers up and down the stem of her wine glass. "Well, you found the pendant. Do you think you're Jessie?" she inquired softly.

Molly gave a short laugh and blushed almost as deeply as the color of the wine. "I know I'm not Jessie, but I am a little envious of her. From these letters, I can tell that Lou loved her so much." She picked up the stack of letters and looked through them. "Jessie's letters are pretty reserved but Lou's, well, that guy had an imagination and a sex drive." Molly laughed.

"I suppose if you knew that you only had a certain amount of time before you'd die, then you'd want to write things that were intimate so the person you were leaving behind wouldn't forget the feelings you had for them when you were gone."

"I suppose," Molly said as she readjusted herself on the couch. "I know if I got letters like that, I'd save them too. They're just so vivid and..." she smiled slightly, "sexual."

"Don't tell me that no one has ever written you a love letter."

Molly laughed shyly at the question. "Well, in grade school or high school maybe, but I've never gotten a real adult R-rated one like Lou wrote, no."

Rowan picked up one of the letters and glanced through it remembering the inspiration for the letter. She was a bit amused that Molly could not see that this letter was clearly written by another woman and smiled at the fact that she was so naive. "Molly, what makes you think Lou was a man?"

"What?" Molly asked at the unexpected question. "Well, he was her lover, and it's a man's name. Why?"

"No reason. I just think you should take a closer look at the letters."

"You think Lou was a woman?" Molly looked at Rowan skeptically, picked up one of the letters, and looked through it. "I don't think so, Rowan."

"Oh, okay." Rowan conceded not wanting to argue a point that really did not matter as far as she was concerned because they had been both in the past.

Molly looked over the letter she was holding and blushed again. "This letter is one of my favorites. It's weird, but I just feel everything when I read this."

Rowan looked curiously at Molly and took the letter from her. She looked at the date and the opening sentence and remembered the event that led to the letter. She smiled and looked mischievously at Molly. "Why don't I read this out loud to you? I'll change the name in it to yours, and it will be like Lou is really talking to you."

Molly laughed at the look on Rowan's face and loved the idea immediately. "Oh, I'd love to hear those words spoken out loud," she teased, "especially with your sexy voice."

"Okay." Rowan smiled and batted her eyes. "Listen closely, Molly. Lou has something to tell you, and the words have been waiting to be said to you for a very long time."

Rowan looked down at the letter as Molly moved closer to her in anticipation of the words of love that would be flowing into her ears. All the wine they had been drinking made Rowan's blood hot and her head swim. She could feel her inhibitions loosen, and she fought for control of the emotions that just wanted to tell Molly how she felt. She wanted to kiss her again.

Rowan took a deep breath to gain some self-control and began speaking softly and sensuously reading the letter using Molly's name as if she were Lou—because she was Lou.

"Molly, being apart from you makes my life feel so hollow. I was lying in my hotel room, and I was with you in my dream last night. I know it was real because our love is so strong no matter how far apart we are in this world.

"Did you feel me in your dream?

"It was raining softly last night while you slumbered. I snuck in on a raindrop to watch you sleep.

"I left a wet kiss on your cheek and another on your nose. I was a bit cold from the rain, so I stripped off my clothes. You looked so warm and content, so I slipped into the bed and wrapped myself around you soaking in some of your warmth. I held you for a long time and finally, I was warm again.

"The feel of your skin and your delicious smell was intoxicating. I couldn't resist so I kissed the side of your neck and your ear. You turned over in your sleep and lay on your back with your arm above your head. You reminded me of Sleeping Beauty, and I wondered if you would wake if I kissed you on your lips. I sat up and leaned over you carefully then ever so gently, I kissed your lips. To my delight, you opened your bright hazel eyes."

Rowan looked up and hoped Molly noticed she changed the eye color to hers. She took another sip of wine and then continued.

"You smiled at the sight of me hovering naked above you. You reached out your hand and stroked my face and hair then grabbed the back of my head and pulled me to you, delivering unto me a deep and sensuous kiss.

"As our bodies pressed against each other, I could feel the heat between your legs, and it sent a buzz of butterflies through my stomach and down where their wings brushed my center gently leaving a want for more of you.

"I saw the slight smile that formed on your lips when you felt what I had ready just for you as I pulled you against myself.

"As we kissed and ran our hands over each other, I managed with great dexterity to remove your pajamas and toss them aside. Naked against each other now, I could feel your warm breasts against me and your arousal against my leg. It filled me with glowing love and excitement that you felt so much desire for me.

"I rolled to your side and pulled you with me so that you were lying on your side, and I put your leg over my hips.

"Open wide to me, I could smell your sweetness, and my head spun at the scent. I moved my hand from your shoulder down along your body and over your breasts and firm nipples, moving closer to you so that I could taste and kiss them. I moved my hand down further slowly and deliberately. I ran it over and around your thigh and then made my way under it and back up where I found your soft curls and ran my fingers through them.

"You moaned in my ear and pushed your hips forward as you ran your hands through my hair and over my body. I parted you with my fingers and slid them along you reveling in the hot liquid that flowed just for me.

"I moved my fingers to your swollen nub and teased it slowly as you grasped me tightly and threw your head back as a low moan left your lips. Your gyrating hips pressed into me, and I could feel your arousal dripping out of you so I moistened the extension of myself with it and kissed you deeply as I pulled myself over you and slid inside you."

Rowan looked up at Molly who had closed her eyes while she was listening. She smiled because it was clear Molly did not understand that only a woman would have a need to use the words 'extension of myself' for a sexual appendage that they were claiming as their own. She looked back down at the letter and continued.

"As I moved in and out of you, slowly and deeply, you clung to me and pulled my hips around in a smooth, undulating rhythm that stirred the senses inside you and filled you with an urgent need for more of me.

"I put my head against yours, and you looked into my eyes. Your face was flushed, your mouth wide open, and your warm breath rushed over my face.

"I quickened my strokes as you pulled me into you wanting more of me, of my passion, of my love.

"With every movement and thought of you, I could feel my arousal building inside as we thrust against each other.

"Suddenly, your breath caught in a soft moan.

"You pushed up against me and clenched me inside you, and you grasped me tightly with your arms and long legs as you let out a cry of rapture. Each of us throbbing around with desire, we held each other tight and kept our slight movement going, an effort to keep the feeling of climax for as long as possible.

"After a while, you began to relax and loosen your hold on me. You looked into my eyes and kissed me tenderly. I began to pull away, and you put your arms around me, 'No,' you pleaded. 'Stay.'

"I smiled and nodded and pushed back into you, and you rewarded me with more sweet caresses and loving kisses.

"Ever so slowly, I pulled away from you and moved my kisses down your body to collect the reward that was mine. The lightest touch of my tongue and breath was all it took to bring out your flavor, which I savored slowly.

"'Lou,' I heard you whisper. 'Please.' You sighed as you arched and writhed as my tongue and nose caressed your delicate nerves.

"You sat up slightly and put your hand under my arms and pulled me up your body. You wrapped yourself around me and pulled my mouth to yours, tasting yourself hungrily.

"Soon, our kisses became so gentle and loving, each one lasting longer and becoming so sweet and tender, until we drifted off into our slumber tangled up in each and this love that is so strong.

"Our love made it through the night and through the rain, keeping us safe in our dream because this love is forever.

"I'll be there with you soon. I miss you, and I love you so very much. I am yours, always. Lou."

The air in the room was thick and warm. Rowan looked up slightly at Molly as she finished the last lines of the letter. She could hear her own heartbeat and Molly's shallow breathing that was so close to her ear.

They were sitting so close together, but it seemed to Rowan they were so far apart. The wine that was coursing through her only enhanced the loving feelings she was having at that moment. The desire was compounded by the images created in her mind and the passion of the words that she had been reading aloud to the woman she loved so deeply.

She turned her head slightly, and she could feel Molly's breath on her lips. She saw the colors in her hazel eyes fade in and out of each other. She was sure they just turned from gold to green near their center. She moved her face slightly closer, losing herself in the wonder of the soul she saw before her.

Hearing those words spoken out loud had such an unexpected effect that Molly felt like she could barely move. The ache running through her body and the warmth of the room were making her light headed. The soft sensual voice was still ringing in her ears and was causing waves of chaos to crash through her mind.

She felt drawn to Rowan in so many ways, and she was feeling like she was going to lose control. She was closer now, just a fraction of an inch, but it felt so much closer.

She wanted to let go, to give in, to lose herself in the warmth she was feeling, but something in her mind was holding her back, making her resist. It was strong, but she fought for what her heart was wanting. She breathed in Rowan's breath, and her eyes closed as she allowed an invisible force to pull her forward.

"Molly!" a loud and angry voice called out followed by and the explosion of banging on the patio door. "Fuck you, Molly! I knew it! I knew it!"

Molly jumped up suddenly in fright and confusion at the unexpected and loud noise. She looked over at the patio door and ran toward it. "Eric? Eric, wait! What? What are you doing here?"

"Eric?" Rowan forced from herself softly as her mind refused to come back to the real world.

Molly slid open the door to a seething Eric and asked her question again. "What are you doing here?"

"What am I doing here? What am I doing here? Catching you fucking around on me, that's what!" Eric shouted as he pointed at the house.

"What are you talking about?" Molly asked as she looked where Eric was pointing. She saw Rowan standing in front of the couch looking a bit confused. "Eric, nothing happened. We were reading the letters I'm turning into a screenplay. That's all."

"Oh, right!" he said as he crossed his arms. "I saw you, Molly! You don't have to be that close just to read a letter."

Rowan cautiously walked to the patio door and smiled her killer smile at Eric still feeling the full effects of all wine she had consumed. "Hi, Eric. Isn't Molly beautiful tonight?"

"Fuck you, Rowan!" he seethed. "I know what you're doing!"

Rowan looked down then around confused. "You do?" she hesitated. "What am I doing?" She smiled.

"You're fucking my girlfriend! That's what you're doing!"

"I am?" she asked confused. Suddenly, she remembered what Molly said about his suspicions and let out a quiet laugh.

"Fuck you!" Eric yelled in her face and turned to leave.

"Eric, wait!" pleaded Molly. "We weren't doing anything!" She explained as she followed him onto the beach.

"Yet," said Rowan softly and laughed to herself. "Unless we already did, and I can't remember," she said worriedly under her breath. So many things were happening, and memories were flooding making it so she couldn't be sure. She saw that Molly was further down on the beach now so she followed her.

"Eric, you're such an unreasonable ass!" Molly shouted. "You're not listening! I'm telling you nothing happened, nothing is happening and nothing will ever happen!"

Rowan looked at Molly and felt her heart tear at her words. "Ever?"

Eric heard Rowan's soft words and was indigent. "So you admit it? I knew it! She's after you, Molly." He tried to compose himself and used his most convincing sales voice. "She's after you, and she'll do anything. She'll do to you what she's done to everyone else she's been with. Is that what you want?"

Molly shook her head confused. "I don't know what you're talking about, Eric. Rowan is my friend. That's all."

"Right! I don't believe that," Eric said sadly. "She wants to seduce you and hurt you just like she does everyone she seduces. She leaves nothing but heartache in her wake."

"I'd never hurt Molly," an annoyed Rowan said, her mind spinning from the wine and words. "She's the one I've been looking for. She's why I'm here."

Eric shook with anger. "Look at her, Molly! She's drunk, and she's still trying to seduce you with me standing here! You've got some nerve, Rowan! Real nerve!"

"Eric, stop! She's just saying that she's helping me with my project. That's all!"

"Fuck you, Molly! You're so stupid, and you're defending her!"

"Don't talk to her like that!" Rowan yelled in Eric's face as she pushed him away from Molly.

Eric pushed her back fuming. "Fuck you too! I'll talk to her any way I want!"

Rowan squinted her eyes and spoke softly but with venom. "Molly should leave you. And she just might if you keep treating her like shit. You're a fucking Philistine!"

"Oh, me? Right!" Eric laughed bitterly. "You're the one who's fucking *my* girlfriend!" In his rage, he turned and began to stomp away.

"That's right. We belong to each other anyway," Rowan said and smiled feeling so happy to say those words out loud.

Molly looked at Rowan wondering what she was talking about, and then turned back toward Eric and watched in horror at the scene that was suddenly unfolding before her.

She heard Eric scream in anger and watched him scoop up a large rock from the beach and hurl it with all the force of his anger at Rowan. She watched it as it sailed through the air. She was certain Rowan would move in time.

Rowan looked up and saw Eric explode into motion and watched as his arm extended. She felt a blinding pain in her head and felt herself fall. Her mind whirled, and she wondered if this was death again.

So soon, she thought.

Too soon, her mind echoed, and the world faded to black.

———

DARKNESS, ALWAYS DARKNESS it seemed to Rowan whenever death was present. The empty feeling of isolation moved its way through her, bringing with it sorrow and disappointment that this soul was still woven into the curse.

It was amazing how much she could still feel, even in death. The cutting pain of loss formed its swirling whirlpool of grief, which spun chaotically as it pulled everything down into its dark and foreboding spiral.

Rowan felt herself reach out into the nothingness and the last blinding pain she felt before her death arose in her again which caused many points of light to appear like a sparkling starry night. She looked at the light with confusion as it began to grow brighter and move closer.

This is new, she thought.

There were a lot of new things happening lately.

Chapter 11

THE IMAGE OF Rowan lying unconscious in the room they had taken her to after she was hit with the rock Eric had thrown at her was still fresh in Molly's mind.

"I'm staying! How could you?" Molly shouted as she burned with anger she had never before felt in her life.

"I said I was sorry! She's fine! She's so drunk, she probably didn't feel a thing!" Eric yelled back as he followed Molly through the house. "So I guess you're sleeping with her. I guess it's all over for us."

Molly turned and looked hotly at Eric. She was amazed at how fast her anger burned away all effects of the wine she drank. "Are you finished? You know, I really thought we would make it through all of this, but I can see that I was a fool. I told you, Rowan is my friend. Why are you suddenly turning into such an ass? Have I been missing something? Have you always been this way? It's like you've suddenly turned into someone else."

"What?" Eric asked contemptuously. "Are you telling me I've changed? Well, I have news for you! You're the one who's changed and not for the better!" he said as he reminded her of her shortcomings. "You're never home anymore, or if you are, you're too busy for me. Then I find out you're spending time alone in a beach house with a notorious lesbian seductress!"

"What?" Molly laughed. "Oh, my god, Eric! You're too much! She is not a seductress!" she said as she waved him off. "See, you just jump to conclusions! The wrong ones I might add!" She looked at him with disbelief and crossed her arms. "So that's what you think of me, that I'd just cheat on you or something? Or is it that you think I can't handle it and say no all by myself if someone makes a move on me? She hasn't, by the way," she said with contempt, "made a move on me. But I think the real problem is that you can't stand that I have a life, and I'm doing things without you."

"You're being ridiculous," said Eric exasperated.

"I can't believe you! Now I'm ridiculous? Every time I try to do something for myself, it seems like you always come up with some reason for me to feel bad about it. Why can't I want to do something for myself?"

"I don't say that. I let you do all kinds of things."

"You let me?" she asked even more annoyed. "Let me? Eric, I don't have to ask you to do this for myself. You're the one who said my screenplay was a waste of time so why should I expect you to understand or help me?"

"Oh, are we on that stupid thing again?"

"Stupid?" she asked as she threw her arms in the air in frustration. "See, there it is. It's not stupid! It's something I feel strongly about doing! Instead of insulting me and my passions, you should be supporting me and encouraging me!"

"Encourage you?" he snorted. "Whatever. I'm telling you it's a waste of your time."

Molly clenched her fists angrily at Eric's obvious amusement. "It's not a waste if it makes me happy. But I guess you don't understand that little point."

"Fine, you know what, you choose one. That stupid screenplay and your good friend Rowan, or me and us. Which is it?"

Stunned at his demand, Molly shook her head in disbelief that he is making her do this again. "No, I can't do that again. Every time you've made me choose, I've chosen you," she said holding back tears of hurt and frustration. "Every time I've chosen you, it seems like I'm the one who becomes more and more unhappy."

"So what are you saying?"

"I guess you'll have to choose this time," she said as she crossed her arms in defiance. "Me, with my screenplay and Rowan, or nothing. I'm not going to stay with you out of misplaced guilt. If you can't deal with me being happy—which includes the things and people that make me happy—then you must not be the one for me." She held his gaze trying not to falter and lose her composure. She swallowed back her fear and discomfort of causing more conflict and made her declaration. "So. Your decision."

"You know what? Fine," he said softly as he placed his hands on Molly's shoulders and then touched her face tenderly. "Do your screenplay, but you can't see Rowan anymore. I love you, and I know she's going to hurt you." He looked sadly into her eyes and whispered. "That's all I ask. Please." He looked into her eyes and whispered, "That's all I ask. Please."

Chapter 12

ROWAN'S WORLD SPUN and a wave of nausea passed through her. She put her hand to her head and then realized—she had a head. That was a good sign. It meant she was not dead yet.

Slowly, she began to open her eyes to the world of the living again. A blurry form hovered over her. The shape moved toward her and then away again and was surrounded by a golden haze of light. Slowly, Rowan's eyes and brain realigned, and her vision began to clear. She lifted her hand that felt so heavy and reached out to the hazy figure and called out softly. "Molly?" She felt the warmth of another hand on hers, and she felt the movement of the bed as the figure sat close beside her.

"You're okay," came a distant voice. "You have a bump, but I think you may mostly just have a hangover."

"What? What happened?" Rowan asked, still trying to see the face of the person beside her. *Did I die again?* Rowan wondered. Molly's voice sounded strange. Was she someone else now? She struggled to regain her vision and focus on the figure before her.

"What happened?" the exasperated voice exclaimed and became clearer. "Well, your crazy girlfriend's crazy boyfriend went crazy! That's what happened!"

"Amy?" Rowan whispered in confusion while fighting back nausea that was threatening to overcome her.

"That's right," she confirmed. "What have I always said about straight girls, especially ones in relationships? Well, okay, pretty much any girl in a relationship?"

Rowan closed her eyes again and let Amy's words roll over her and the nausea ease. Amy was never at a loss for words and rarely kept her feelings a secret. They met when Rowan was hired at the gallery and Amy came in to do an interview for the magazine where she worked. They dated for a short time, but Rowan knew they would be better off as friends. Better off because Rowan was already searching for the pendant and Jessie.

Rowan told Amy how she felt and that, though she cared for her, she knew they weren't meant to be together. It did not go well at first because Amy protested dramatically and loudly, but after a while, it seemed as though Amy understood, and she worked to just be a friend. Since then, they had become close and caring friends.

Rowan could do nothing at the moment but let the compulsive advice-giver go on with her speech. When there was finally a break, she opened her eyes and asked softly, "Molly?"

Amy sighed when she saw the hopefulness in Rowan's eyes knowing that the hope was in vain. "She," Amy paused, "she's not here, Rowan."

"Where is she?"

"She left."

"Left?"

"That's right," she said as she rubbed Rowan's arm to try and soothe her. "You're just lucky I'm the first name in your cell phone because I'm the only person whose name begins with an A that you know."

Rowan smirked sadly up at her friend. "Hmmm, I guess I'll have to remedy that."

"Yeah, you do that. Anyway, I was the first name in your phone, and she recognized my name from the gallery party so she called me. What the hell is going on with you lately, Rowan?" asked Amy.

"You wouldn't understand," Rowan replied as she lightly felt the small lump on her head. "Did she leave with him? Did she say she'd be back? What happened?"

"Rowan," said Amy softly, "she was alone when I got here. She told me about her crazy rock-throwing boyfriend, and she just kept saying she was sorry over and over again. She packed up all her things and left."

"Oh," whispered Rowan wishing Molly hadn't gone. She was confused as to the reason she had decided to go. "I guess she went back with him."

Amy looked at the sadness that covered Rowan's face like a shadow and sighed heavily. "Rowan, it'll be okay. You don't need to be with some chick with a crazy rock guy for a boyfriend." She looked at Rowan and hesitated, trying not to show her own pain and jealousy that Rowan did not have feelings for her anymore.

Then, ever the journalist asked the hard question. "Do you really love her?"

Looking up at Amy, and without hesitation, Rowan confirmed her feelings. "Yes, from the very first moment I saw her. She haunts my life," Rowan whispered, "my thoughts and my dreams. I know she's part of me. We're connected. I can feel it all the time. But will we ever find our way to each other? That is the real question."

Chapter 13

THE STRANGE SENSATION reaching Molly's ears ran through her dream and sent vibrations through her similar to that of a freight train speeding down its tracks and shaking the earth. The air around her was sucked away taking with it first her breath and then her body. Taken up quickly from the ground by the twisting winds, she tumbled through the ripping and angry air.

Suddenly, she was caught in its calm eye as earth, water, and debris circled her, making it impossible for her to see outside its swirling walls. Fears from her youth penetrated her body making her heart beat hard as she recognized the tornado as it swept her away. For so many years, she lived with her grandmother's fear of tornadoes, and even now that she lived so far away from her mid-western home, her subconscious held onto the fear of her youth.

She floated in the calm eye for what seemed an eternity as the predacious winds howled and screamed. She overcame her panic and made herself look closer at the many things that swirled just outside her reach. She was surprised by what she saw.

Images and words appeared and then emotions and feelings sparked colorful explosions causing the winds to spin faster and made the thunder even louder. It was then, as she looked closely at the images, she realized where she was and what was happening.

She was witnessing the whirlwind of thoughts and emotions that were tormenting her mind. The journals and letters had been consuming her time and her emotions. Her life was revolving in the powerful force that surrounded her.

She struggled to reach out for the pages that were whirling around her, but she was caught in a calm place where she was trapped and had no way of getting to them. Her frustration grew as she fought against her prison, but there was no escape.

Molly closed her eyes against the tears that threatened to escape, and when she opened them, the world had changed again. Darkness and silence were all around her. She panicked and closed her eyes again. When she opened them, she could see that her new surroundings were familiar. She was in the beach house where she was before with Rowan. She desperately and frantically looked for Rowan's heart to keep it safe and hold it together. She was not sure why she had to do it, but the compulsion made the task seem very urgent.

She came to a door that she instinctively felt was Rowan's, her confusion growing because it was not the same door she remembered. It was a doorway she had never been to before. She was bewildered and panicked again. She pounded on the door and twisted the door handle as she called out, "Rowan? Rowan, I'm here!"

Her heart pounded in her chest as she grasped the door handle twisting it and pushing against the door. She was taken by surprise and stumbled into the room as the latch released and the door opened. She caught herself and was able to find her balance as she surveyed the dark room.

She saw Rowan's sleeping form, a darker shadow in the night, lying on the bed. Relief flooded through her as she made her way to her and knelt beside the bed. She allowed time for her eyes to adjust to the low light of the moon that had made its way into the room.

As her eyes adjusted, she looked down at Rowan. Her beautiful face stained with tears and, even in sleep, holding onto a furrowed brow against the pain and heartache that gripped her. "Oh, Rowan," she whispered as tears flowed down her own cheeks. "I'm so sorry. I've been so worried about you. Things are so hard and confusing. I'm not sure what to do."

Rowan turned her head toward Molly and opened her shining eyes. She looked up and wiped a tear from Molly's face. "Hey, you're back," she said softly. "I'm so glad you're here. I missed you, and I've been calling for you."

Molly's worried face transformed and brightened as she looked down at Rowan and smiled. "I'm glad you're okay. You can't imagine how much I've been worrying about you."

"Please, don't worry. You're so wonderful. This is just a new beginning, a new journey. A journey I hope to take with you."

Molly reached out to put her hand on Rowan's face to check if she was real even though she could sense that she was dreaming. She touched Rowan's face and winced at the sight of the bump on her head.

"Does it hurt? It all happened so fast, and when I saw you fall, I..."

Rowan pulled her down gently and kissed her sweetly. Molly pulled away, looked into Rowan's eyes, and saw only love glowing from them under the light of the moon. She pulled back the blanket that covered Rowan.

"Scoot over, let me in. I want to hold you."

Rowan pouted and sighed. "I hate this damn bed. It's so small and uncomfortable." She moved and let Molly in, and she pulled her close. Rowan put her leg between Molly's and pulled Molly's leg over her hips and then kissed her again.

"It's okay, babe. We'll just have to stay close together all night and use each other for a little comfort." Molly ran her hands over Rowan and kissed her again hoping to ease her pain. Soon, Rowan's kisses strayed to Molly's jaw and up to her ear, and her hands moved smoothly over her body.

Molly sighed and turned her head so that she was looking into Rowan's eyes again. "Rowan, I'm sorry. I'm just... I don't know if I can. Please, will you just hold me?"

Rowan nodded. "I'll hold you and kiss you," she said as she continued to do just that. She ran her hands under Molly's shirt and over her soft, warm skin. "I want to show you how much I love you. I want to take away as much hurt as I can. I want to carry some of your burdens."

Molly took a breath, and she wanted to say something about her being the one who should be taking away the hurt, but she stopped herself. Instead, she sighed and closed her eyes as Rowan moved her kisses to her neck, her hand brushing lightly over her breasts. Molly could feel her own nipples harden and knew that even though her mind was telling her she couldn't, her body ached to be touched, and her heart needed to drink the love pouring out of Rowan.

"I love you, Molly," Rowan whispered then kissed her deeply.

They lost themselves in their kiss for the longest time, comforted by the taste of each other and their closeness.

Thoughts and emotions whirled through Molly's mind like the tornado she had arrived in. She felt a comfort and peace she had never known, but at the same time, an underlying fear of the unknown made her body shake and her breathing shallow.

Her heart took charge of the logic that her mind was trying to force through and tossed it aside like an empty promise. They broke apart for air and Molly whispered huskily into Rowan's ear. "I love you too, so much."

They fell into each other again groping and pulling at each other's clothing wanting to be closer, to feel so much more of each other.

Molly felt as if she should say something, but she stayed silent, her desire stopping the flow of her thoughts to her lips.

Rowan moved her hand down between Molly's legs and into her panties. She slid her fingers through Molly and over her clit down to the edge of her and back again.

"My, god, Rowan. What are you doing to me?" Molly moaned as the sensation rippled through her body. Molly moved her hips to meet Rowan's fingers, and she pulled her closer finding her lips again.

Rowan pressed her fingers into Molly, slowly moving them in circles over her clit and down to feel the wetness that was forming at her touch. Molly's need grew quickly, and soon, Rowan's hand was covered in Molly, her fingers wet, slick, and ready to move inside her. She entered her slowly but going as deep as she could before pulling out then pushing in again.

"Oh, Rowan," Molly burst out then buried her head in Rowan's neck.

Rowan kept her fingers deep inside Molly, curling and probing slowly, carefully and lovingly while she kept her thumb pressed on her clit.

Molly began moving her hips matching and then demanding another rhythm from Rowan. Faster, deeper, harder.

But Rowan purposely held back, prolonging the pleasure she knew Molly was feeling and wanting to last. She wanted Molly's body to memorize the sensation and imprint it in her mind.

Molly's mind and body were coming undone. Every nerve in her body was on fire with a passion so new and powerful that she knew it could only become an addiction she could never break. Her closeness, her touch, her scent, her body, her love, her. Rowan. Her Rowan.

"I need more," Molly pleaded. "Please."

Rowan could hear the need in her voice and let Molly set the rhythm. She rocked against Molly as she thrust toward her and gripped her tightly.

Molly could feel Rowan's fingers moving deep inside her. Her hand rubbed against her and her clit, banging into it fast, hard, deep.

"Oh," Molly gasped, and she felt herself clench around Rowan's fingers, but she kept moving inside her. "God," Molly moaned just as her body trembled with release, and she flowed over Rowan's warm hand.

She felt Rowan's mouth cover hers again with the warmth of her body against her. A tingling sensation rushed through her followed by a sudden wave of calm that flowed over her. She put her head against Rowan's and looked into her eyes and saw her soul and how far it had traveled to be with her.

Rowan gave her a small smile, remembering how uncertain Molly had been just a short time ago, and whispered softly, "I guess you can, just a little."

Molly gave her a small laugh and kissed her lips, her nose, her eyelids, and said, "I want to stay like this all night, babe." She reached down and put her hand over Rowan's that was still inside her. "Yes, I want you like that. I love you."

Rowan smiled at her words and whispered, "I love you too, very much. Let's start planning our journey now. I want to be with you always."

Wet and aching, Molly woke up from her dream to the sound of the phone ringing. She put the pillow over her face to wipe away her tears of frustration and to block out the offensive sound of the phone. Eventually, it stopped and rolled into voice mail. She was fairly sure she knew who it was and knew she was in no state to talk with anyone right now.

He had been calling almost every day for the last month. She told Eric that she needed time—time to figure out what she wanted and time to work on her screenplay without interruption. He honored that for about a week.

What she did not tell him was that she needed time to figure out her feelings for Rowan. Molly had barely gotten any work done because, every time she started reading those damn letters, she could not help thinking about Rowan and what she felt when Rowan was reading her that letter. Thoughts about the small kiss in Rowan's office and about how she felt when she saw Rowan get hurt while defending her kept resurfacing, too.

Then there were the dreams. God, they were so real. She would wake up aching and trembling. Her chest would feel like it was being squeezed by an invisible hand. She stopped herself several times a day from contacting Rowan and fought the compulsion to just drop everything and run to her. It was draining her of all her energy. *How could I miss someone this much who I barely know*, she wondered.

She sighed heavily and brought her arm and the pillow down from her face to her side. She looked over at the bedside table at her phone and dreaded listening to another one of Eric's voice mails. She groaned knowing she just had to get it over with so she reached over to pick up the phone. She dialed into her voice mail and waited with trepidation for the message to begin.

"Hey, Molly. It's Rowan." The voice hesitated. "I'm sorry. I know you said you needed a break from hanging out with me, but, well, I need to talk with you. It...it's about the letters... uh... your screenplay. I really need to talk to you soon. I hope you call... or you can just come to Valoria's. I'll be there for a while this afternoon... and maybe some tomorrow. If you don't catch me there, I don't live far... so... well... just call me, and I'll give you the address. Maybe you could bring the letters. It really is important."

Molly lowered the phone slowly from her ear and swallowed back her surprise. "Fuck," she said softly. She thought Rowan had just decided she was too much to deal with and hated her now because of what Eric had done.

Then there was what she did. She didn't tell her she needed a break. She did something that was much more hurtful. She didn't know if she could face her. Not after that, not now, not with all the dreams she had been having about her and all the—thoughts.

She dropped the phone on the bed and wiped her sweaty palms on the sheets. She couldn't believe how just hearing her voice made her this nervous. She had never felt like this before.

What that hell is wrong with me, she thought.

CHapter 14

ROWAN LOOKED CLOSELY at her computer screen, made a few corrections, and then concentrated on getting every thought she typed as clear and detailed as possible.

The crowd and the noise in the restaurant seemed far away, and in her sight, she could only see the images in her mind and the words she used to describe them. She was fulfilling Jessie's request. She was recording all of her memories of their past lives. She already had several completed and printed out to give to Molly. She wasn't sure how many she would be able to get done before… no, she wasn't going to think about that right now.

She was determined to complete as much as she could. She had a mission to try to prove to Molly who they were, who they are, and that all of this is real.

"Whatcha doin'?" asked Amy as she stood over Rowan and smiled.

Rowan looked up and came back into the present world. She watched while Amy and their friend Shannon pulled their chairs up to the table. "Hi, Amy. Hey, Shannon," she said and closed the window she had been working in. "I'm just working on a project."

"Oh," Amy said and picked up one of the envelopes on the table reading it as she sat and wrinkling her brow. "Last Will and Testament?"

Shannon looked up at Rowan. "Is there something going on your friends should know about?"

Rowan took the envelope from Amy's hand. "No, just being prepared."

Amy looked suspiciously at her. "What's going on? You've been…" she hesitated, "well, weird lately." She looked at the other envelope and saw it had Molly's name on it. "Oh, my god!"

Shannon looked up. "What?"

Amy picked up the envelope. "Molly? What the hell, Rowan? She hasn't talked to you in like a month. Are you still…" she shook her head. "I mean you're not, you don't think? Rowan! What the hell are you doing?"

Rowan sighed and shook her head. "It's nothing, Amy. It's for her screenplay."

A sharp jab of jealousy pierced into Amy. "You still love her." It was not a question, but a fact she could see was true. "Rowan, why are you doing this to yourself? She's out there with 'crazy rock guy' doing who knows what and living her life, and you're here doing what? Helping her with her screenplay? That's so fucked! You need help."

Rowan snapped closed her computer. "Thanks, Amy."

"Seriously, you have to forget about her and move on. That Eric guy was serious when he told you to step off. Maybe that rock to the head really messed you up!"

"Yeah, the guy sounds like a real piece of work," Shannon added.

Rowan looked into Amy's eyes with an unwavering gaze. "So you think I should just walk away from the person I know I'm supposed to be with? The person who is the other half of my soul, the person I have no doubt is the 'one'?"

Amy was flustered. "But, Rowan. She's gone. She just walked away without a word to you. She's…" she reigned in her anger. "I'm sorry, but she's a fucking coward."

Rowan shook her head. "No, Amy. She's not a coward. I'm sure it took a lot of strength and bravery to give up a friend. She gave up someone she felt a connection to and who made her happy."

"Whatever! Rowan, you need to find someone who you know loves you, and someone who'll be here for you. You can't live in some kind of wishful fantasy world forever!"

Rowan smiled sadly and bit her lip. "Someone like you, Amy?"

"Whoa! I'm outta here, girls! This sounds like it's getting personal. Later!" Shannon got up and walked over to another table of friends.

"I'm here, Rowan," Amy said as she pouted and began to fidget with her nails.

"I know, and I'm glad you are. But Amy, I know I'm meant for her. Just like I know there's someone out there who's meant just for you, too. But it's not me. I'm sorry."

Tears welled up in Amy's eyes and one broke loose. "How do you know that?" she whispered.

Rowan wiped away Amy's tear wishing she could tell her all the things she knew without sounding like a lunatic. She always knew when she found the other half of her soul, the one she loved so completely and who she had lived so many lives for, the one she worked to be with for an entire lifetime. She would love to tell her about the times she saw souls find each other that were meant to be together. It was the most beautiful and wonderful thing to see, and it was something so tragic when the souls were pulled apart by the oppression of the physical world.

Rowan sighed. "I just know. I feel that unmistakable connection to her."

Amy gathered herself and sniffed bravely. "Well, if it were me, I'd hate her and never see her again. Someone who's supposed to be your soul mate wouldn't do that to you."

"Oh, Amy. You wouldn't hate her. You couldn't."

"Oh, ho! Yes, I could!"

Rowan gave a soft laugh. "Amy, you have too much spirit and love inside you. You'd find a way to remain in her life. You'd probably do it in some completely crazy way, but you'd never really hate her."

Amy looked down and considered Rowan's words. "Maybe. Why is it so hard? I could be happy with you, really. I feel connected to you, I do."

"I'm sure you could, but don't you want more than that?" Rowan took Amy's hand and looked into her eyes. "Amy, you, everyone, deserves to be with someone who loves them back totally. If I gave up on Molly and went with you, not only would I be unhappy, but also, eventually, my unhappiness would cause us problems, and then you'd become unhappy, too. I don't want to make you unhappy. Just keep being my friend. Know that I do love you as a friend, and the connection you feel for me, I feel for you. But I also know that what I feel is just friendship."

Amy broke eye contact with Rowan and sighed. "Okay. Sorry." She looked up, and just as Rowan was about to speak, she cut her off. "Holy shit! Speak of the devil!"

Rowan turned and looked toward the front of the restaurant where she saw Molly. She was standing nervously at the door running her hand over the back of her neck and through her hair. "Oh, she got my message."

"You, you called her? Rowan, 'rock guy' is gonna go ballistic!"

Rowan winked at Amy. "It's a chance I'll have to take." She stood up and waved at Molly.

"I'm outta here," Amy declared and started toward the table where her friend Shannon was sitting.

———————

MOLLY SAW ROWAN stand as she made her way to her table, passing Amy on the way. She could not look into Amy's eyes, and she saw the dislike that was so clear on her face. She hesitated and felt the blood rush to her face. Before she realized it, she was standing in front of Rowan looking into her liquid brown eyes that seemed to see right into her.

"Hi," Rowan said quietly. "I'm glad you made it."

Molly found it hard to speak and pushed down the thought of wanting to feel Rowan's lips on hers again.

"Hi." She had to fight this. She was sure she couldn't do this, and her mind clashed against her heart. "So, you said you wanted to talk to me about my screenplay and it was important?"

"That's right. Sit down." She motioned to the chair across from her, and they both sat. Rowan picked up the envelope with Molly's name on it holding it in both hands as she looked up into Molly's eyes. "First, I do realize everything I'm about to tell you is going to sound crazy. I just want you to know that if you just hear me out, you'll see I'm telling you the truth." She could see that Molly was nervous and confused. "Molly, I love you."

"Wh—what?" Molly was stunned. This definitely was not what she had expected to hear, and she felt slightly panicked. She fought back the thoughts and the memories of the dreams she had about

Rowan. They were wrong—they had to be. She was not a lesbian. She stood suddenly not really knowing what to say or to do.

"No, Rowan. I—I have to go."

Rowan watched Molly walk out of the restaurant and felt her own heart skid into a heaping wreck in her chest.

"So, you told her?" asked Amy as she sat down next to Rowan.

"Yes," Rowan said as she sadly packed up her things to leave.

Chapter 15

IT HAS BEEN said that it never rains in California, but today, the heavens opened up and proved that saying wrong. The warm rain started without much warning and fell heavily from the suddenly darkened sky as it pounded relentlessly on the car.

Inside the car, a rain of tears, filled with uncertainty and frustration, trailed down red and puffy cheeks, under a quivering chin and into the small hollow of Molly's neck. It didn't matter how hard she tried to hold back the tears or how often she wiped them away, they came uncontrollably like rain from her eyes. The combination of the rain and all her tears made it hard for her to see the road ahead, so she pulled over to give them both time to run themselves out.

She put the car in park, and all of her emotions came to a head. There was nothing for her to do but let the tears flow. She breathed in short gasps as she leaned her head against the steering wheel and gripped and pulled on it in frustration and anger. She was feeling frustration because of the feelings she was having and feeling anger because she just could not make them stop.

Slowly, her heart calmed, and she was able to take several deep breaths. She looked into the rearview mirror and wiped her red and puffy eyes.

"God, I look like shit," she said quietly to herself.

Looking into her own eyes, she could see the fear and anxiety in them and tears started to slowly leak out again.

"I have to stop this!" she cried out to the mirror. "I have to stop," she told herself as she leaned her head against the steering wheel.

In her mind, she could see Rowan as she said the words 'I love you.' It was just like in her dreams. Her mind and heart were at odds with each other—one with joy and the other with fear. She took another deep, shuddering breath and brought herself under some semblance of control. She stopped crying. She now had that under control too, or maybe she had just run out of tears for the moment. Whichever it was, she felt she should take advantage of it and try to get the car moving again. The further she drove away from Rowan and the more she thought about how she left things in the restaurant, the more Molly felt the grip of remorse.

She looked through the rain-covered windshield, listened to the rhythm of the windshield wipers, and made her decision. She turned the car around and headed back to the restaurant to find Rowan.

The short run from the car to the restaurant left Molly drenched and dripping. She scanned the tables looking for Rowan but couldn't see her through the crowd of people who had come in to escape the rain.

"What are you doing back?" asked a voice behind Molly.

Molly turned quickly and came face to face with Amy who looked at her with disdain. "I—I'm looking for Rowan."

"Well, she isn't here," said Amy hotly as she crossed her arms.

"Oh, do you know where she is?"

"Maybe. Why?"

Uncomfortable under Amy's scrutiny, she answered softly. "I—" she stammered, "I need to talk to her."

Amy squinted as she looked at Molly. "I don't understand. You left. You just up and left. Now you're back?"

"I know," Molly tried to explain nervously.

Amy interrupted her, not really interested in what she had to say as she allowed her anger to ooze. "Quite a pattern you have there. What is this?" She pretended to think. "Oh, yeah. It's the second time you've just left with barely a word. You going for a third time?" she asked sarcastically.

Amy's sarcasm was not lost on Molly, and she spoke nervously and quietly. "I'm sorry. I just need to talk to Rowan… to explain."

"Explain?" Amy said as she shook her head. "Let's see, Rowan tells you she loves you… you walk out. I don't think there's much to explain." She brushed past Molly and made her way to the back of the restaurant.

Molly turned and followed her. "You don't understand."

Amy stopped short and turned to face her making Molly nearly run into her. "Oh, I don't understand?" she asked and put her hands on her hips. "You know, you should have just kept moving and not come back. I think you've done enough damage, and I'm sure Rowan doesn't need you to explain a thing."

"Please," Molly pleaded and looked at Amy with red-rimmed eyes. "Amy, I need you to tell me her address. I didn't mean to hurt her. I never wanted that. Please, tell me her address."

"You're fucking kidding me, right?"

Molly swallowed back her tears. "No."

"So, what are you going to do? Go over and twist the knife?" She began to turn away again, not waiting for Molly to answer.

"Amy, wait. No. I don't want to do that. I just need to talk to her. Tell her I still want to be her friend. But I'm not, I can't," she said softly then looked down as her face flushed with embarrassment at the words she was about to say out loud, and then she blurted them out. "I'm not a lesbian."

Amy looked at Molly with incredulity and shook her head. "I don't think you need to explain that. I think she gets the picture of exactly how you feel about her."

"Wait, what?" Molly asked in surprise.

"Well, let's see. You let your 'rock guy' practically kill her, and you go running back to his crazy ass, leaving Rowan lying unconscious practically on her own after walking out without a word." She took an impatient breath. "When she finally woke up and asked about you, I had to tell her you took off. Yeah, great friend!" She rolled her eyes. "Then you don't talk to her for a month. Now, there's true friendship. Meanwhile, Rowan spends time helping you with your screenplay because," she shook her head in frustration, "well, obviously, she feels something for you. So when she gets up the nerve to call you and tell you how she's feeling, you do it again! You just pick up and walk out. You're not a friend, lesbian or not! So stop trying to fool everyone and just go home!"

"I am her friend," Molly whispered softly.

"Right. Do you know how many people she's actually told she loves?"

Molly looked down and swallowed. "No."

"Including you, one. Get it?" she said curtly while struggling to keep her jealousy under control. She turned to walk away again.

Molly was speechless as she watched Amy walk away. She shook off her shock at Amy's words and followed her. She touched Amy's arm to get her attention. "But, she... she's had lots of—"

"Of what? Lovers? You keep believing that. I know the rumors are out there, and I'm not saying she hasn't had some, but most are just that, rumors. They just make them up because she's so private.

People like to think they know everything, and when they don't, they start rumors." Amy looked at Molly with disgust. "Rowan isn't some seductress like your rock guy thinks! She's not. She's just not!" Amy continued in a rage. "You're responsible for hurting her physically, mentally, and emotionally, in every fucking way possible!"

Molly wiped a drip of water from her face, unsure if it was a tear of anger or a drip of rain from her hair. "I'm sorry," she whispered, and it was all she could manage as she held in her emotions.

"I'll bet," replied Amy her voice dripping with sarcasm. "Great friend!"

"But I—"

"What? You what? You didn't mean to? What a load of shit! I'm her real friend! Just admit it. You're not her friend! You hate her because of some heterophobic bullshit, and her feelings and emotions mean nothing to you!"

"I don't hate her," Molly said beginning to shake with anger.

"Well, you're too late! She doesn't want you for a friend anyway! She wants more, and you won't or can't give her what she wants! You walked out, and now she's gone! You lost your chance to be anything to her! You don't deserve her, and you certainly don't deserve another chance! She needs someone who really cares! Someone who loves her!"

"I—" was all that Molly could stammer before Amy let loose on her again.

"You? You what? You have to go again? Fine! There's the door!" Amy pointed. "Rowan is not sub-human or some toy for you to play games with! I can't believe she loves you! You're just, just pathetic! 'I'm not a lesbian,'" Amy mocked. "Jesus! Is that the best you can come up with to tell her? Just face it—she doesn't need you. She doesn't need you to explain or make her understand. You're the one who walked out! You've lost your chance to *explain*. She gets it. You don't really like her! You certainly don't love her!"

"But I—" started Molly her anger at Amy's words building inside her because she wasn't listening or letting her talk.

"You what? What? Come on, Molly! Explain it to me, and please make it a better reason than you've come up with so far! You what?" Amy waited for Molly's answer with her hands on her hips.

Seething with anger and fear and panic, Molly shouted her answer that was based on pure raw emotion that came from deep within her soul. "I love her!"

Amy stared back at Molly with shock and disbelief.

Silence washed over both women as Molly put her hand over her mouth. Her eyes were wide as she stared at Amy, and her body shook with the realization of why she had been in such turmoil.

———————

LOVE, TRUE LOVE, should never ever be something taken for granted. It should be acknowledged every day, every moment, and it should be known that this love is there without question, doubt, or hesitation.

Make sure that the words 'I love you' are heard in a soft whisper or a joyful laugh, or seen every day whether written by hand in a special note or just a quick text or felt in passion or in the passing of a gentle touch. Each day in life, the knowledge of love should be known absolutely.

Having the knowledge of true love, emotionally, physically, spiritually and intellectually, is a gift that is more valuable than anything on this earth. No matter what, no matter how bad things are or how hard things are sometimes, true love is the one thing you can count on, is undeniable, unwavering, and unconditional.

True love is the difference between just loving someone and being in love with someone. It is what makes lovers lay their lives down for each other and make heroic sacrifices.

True love is life. It is eternal life for those who find it within themselves to allow it in and recognize it for what it is when it finds them.

Molly was allowing it in today. She finally recognized what her soul had been aching and fighting for all this time. It was not an easy thing to acknowledge. It was terrifying.

She had never known anything like this before, and it made her physically weak. Just the thought of being too late made her feel sick, and her stomach turned. The rampage of emotions inside her blinded her to everything and made her deaf to the sounds around her. She was guided to the address Amy had given her by pure intuition and by the fortune gifted to her by the fates.

So many things ran through her mind as logic and emotion fought each other. Her head spun with questions and self-doubt.

What if her soul could not overcome the limitations and worries in her mind? What if her view of security and her concept of the standards of living she grew up with prevented her from going where her heart wanted to go? What if she panics and runs away again like Amy thinks she will? Molly opened her car door and stepped out into the pouring rain. She looked up at Rowan's front door, and it looked so far away. Soaked through with rain, she did not feel the dampness or the cold. Her anticipation and insecurity burned through her as she took her first step toward an uncertain future.

Chapter 16

I AM THE forgotten one. I remember everything that you never can. I have to start again with you each time because my memories are complete but yours are not. We are always different… always someone new but with the same souls somehow.

Riddles and magic rule all of my lives, and I fight on for the life I dream of with you.

I am eternally yours, and you are mine. This fact is what keeps me living these lives and searching for you, in hopes that someday we will have what was denied to us so long ago—a lifetime together.

ROWAN STOPPED TYPING and rubbed her throbbing temples. She could feel her heart struggling to beat inside her chest. The loss and pain never got any easier to bear.

The look of fear on Molly's face when she told her that she loved her seemed to cement her fate. This life was coming to an end without much of an opportunity to reveal the truth to Molly.

The days had been slipping away so quickly and now the hours were filled with despair, and there were too few of them left. There was nothing left to do now but carry on with Jessie's last request and hope that when Molly received the information, she would carry on

Jessie's work. Or at the very least, she would make sure the papers were kept with the pendant so they could be found again in their next lives.

It was the hardest decision she could remember making—to choose between Jessie's request and going after Molly. But the little time she had left helped her see that she needed to use the time in the best way possible, and that was to do the one thing that could help them both break the curse.

Rowan looked up at the calendar and saw that she had only weeks to complete as much as she could. There were mere weeks until her life would once again come to an end, and this time without even a chance at solving the riddle or an attempt to break the curse. She put her hands back on the keyboard to continue revealing all of the lives that had been entwined in their curse.

Rowan looked up from her computer screen puzzled by the soft knocking on the door. She sighed at the interruption and got up to answer the door.

The sight that met Rowan's eyes as she opened the door was both heartbreaking and monumentally joyful. Heartbreaking because she could see the uncertainty and fear on Molly's face. It was a face that was surrounded by dripping wet blonde hair darkened from the rain, and her eyes and her cheeks were ruddy from crying.

Rowan could see Molly's body shaking from a mix of holding back her emotions and the chill of the water that had soaked through her clothes to her skin. All of those things Rowan could see, but in spite of them, the feeling of elation filled her at the unexpected and wonderful sight of the one she loved.

Even though Rowan's heart and soul were filled with delight, she fought to control herself and spoke cautiously. "Hi," she said softly not wanting to do or say anything to make Molly walk away again.

Molly looked down at the pool of water that had formed under her feet. "Hi," was all she could manage as she shifted nervously. She swallowed some of her fear and looked up into Rowan's eyes. "Rowan, I'm sorry," she said softly. "I shouldn't have walked away. We," she sniffed, "we need to talk."

Rowan stood in the doorway barely hearing Molly's words for the rush of feelings and hopeful thoughts that were running through her mind. She blinked as Molly's words made it to the front of her mind and were translated into something she could understand.

"Oh, okay. Come in," she stammered and led Molly into the house. "Why don't I get you a towel so you can dry off?" she offered as Molly followed her silently to into the hall. "Ah, well, here's the bathroom. Maybe you should just go in and dry off. I'll wait out here."

"Thank you," she said as she entered the bathroom. "I... I'm sorry," she said again as she looked back at the trail of water she tracked through the house.

"It's okay," Rowan replied almost automatically as the bathroom door closed. She went to the kitchen with a dazed smile on her face, grabbed the mop, and cleaned up the water Molly had left behind.

She returned to the bathroom door and knocked lightly. "Molly. You can use my blow dryer if you want. It's in the cabinet."

"Thanks," a muffled voice came back from the other side of the door. "Rowan?"

"Yes?" Rowan answered and inside her heart, she knew 'yes' was the answer to so much more.

"Do you think, well, do you think you could put my clothes in your dryer?"

Rowan smiled and laughed softly as she leaned against the wall next to the door. "Yes," she said, so happy that she had another chance to spend time with this woman. She heard Molly moving around, and soon, the door opened just a crack.

"Rowan?"

"Yes?" she replied again wanting to tell her so badly that she could have all of her heart and soul.

"Here are my clothes," Molly said as she handed the soaking wet clothes through the slight opening of the door. "I'm sorry."

"Molly, you don't have to keep saying you're sorry."

"Sorry."

Rowan smiled again at Molly's reply and took the wet clothes from her. The door gently snapped shut, and Rowan knocked lightly. "If you need to you can use the shower and warm up. You can use my robe while your clothes dry. I'll bring it to you." She turned and took the clothes to the dryer.

———

INSIDE THE BATHROOM, Molly was wrapped in one of the oversized towels she found hanging neatly on the towel rack. She looked into the mirror at her reflection. Her mind reeled in disbelief at what she was doing.

She was about to tell this woman that she loved her.

She had already confessed it to Amy.

Now she found herself standing naked in a strange bathroom. She looked like shit. At the knock on the bathroom door, she gasped, jumped nervously, and turned toward the voice.

"Molly, I'm setting the robe outside the door for you. You can get it when you're ready. Take your time," Rowan gently told her.

"Thank you," she replied softly as she leaned against the door. Hearing Rowan move away, she slowly opened the door and picked up the robe that was left for her.

With a sigh, Molly hung the robe on the hook by the shower. She turned on the water in the shower and sat on the toilet lid to wait for the water to warm. When steam made its way from the shower, Molly took off her towel and hung it on the towel rack.

She stepped carefully into the warm and gently falling water. It warmed her body as it tumbled down and over her head to her face where it had formed streams that meandered down her neck and over her chest to her breasts and flowed out and off of her like a waterfall. She let out a long, slow breath and opened her eyes looking for the soap. She poured the soap over the shower sponge and rubbed it with her hand to create lather then ran the soap-laden sponge over her body creating thick foaming trails. The scent of the soap brought images of Rowan to her mind, and she could feel her body react as she ran her hands over herself.

Flashing images and confusing thoughts filled her mind, and they led to questions that led to more questions. *How do you love a woman? What do I do first? How different is it, really? What the hell am I doing?*

She looked down at herself and moved her hand over the golden curls between her legs. *Does Rowan feel like this, too? Would she feel the same sensation?* Molly took a soft quivering breath as the tip of her finger rubbed against her clit. "God," she moaned as her mind reeled at the soft, moist feeling and the ache that it caused as she ran her fingers through her soft folds. Then all she could think of was how Rowan would react or if she would like what she was feeling. "Rowan," she said out loud yet softly.

"Molly?"

Molly's eyes snapped open, and she jumped at the sound of the knock and Rowan's voice. "What?" was all she could weakly manage.

"Are you okay?" Rowan asked through the closed door.

Molly stood up and bit her lip nervously. "Fuck," she whispered. "I'm fine. Fine," she said loud enough for Rowan to hear. She could feel her face burning with embarrassment. "What the hell am I doing?" she asked herself quietly.

"Oh, I thought I heard you say my name, so I thought you needed something," Rowan said with concern. "Since it's lunch time, I've made you a little something to eat."

"Oh, okay, thanks. I'll be out in just a bit," Molly said as she rushed to rinse off the soap and finish washing her hair. She turned off the water and grabbed the towel to wrap around herself.

Chapter 17

THE RAIN TAPPED its heavy melody upon the windows and the roof as Rowan carried two wine glasses into the living room. She set them on the coffee table next to the chilled bottle of wine. Beside them were two plates of sandwiches and fruit. Centered between the plates was a large brown envelope with Molly's name written on it topped by white sheets of neatly stacked printed pages.

Rowan looked over the arrangement carefully and made a few slight adjustments because she wanted everything to be perfect. She was very excited that Molly was there. She could hardly contain herself as she looked down the hallway with a smile that was filled with happiness and love.

All the waiting, searching, and patience had come to this moment in time. This time when, once again, she must choose to tell her everything or choose to let her live a life without knowing the truth. Rowan knew that her time was very short. If she told Molly everything, it may all end in disaster. The pain it might cause Molly would be less if the truth were kept from her. But keeping the truth from her meant losing the chance at living a life together now.

Rowan looked at the envelope and papers on the table. Her smile turned into a frown of uncertainty, and she picked up the papers. Maybe she should wait. Maybe it was too late to start all of this now.

She put her other hand to her head as it spun with indecision and memories that flashed through her mind.

Fears of losing this chance and causing Molly pain clashed in her heart, and she held back the tears that wanted to form. Before she had time to take the papers away, she heard the door down the hall open and Molly coming toward her. She turned and watched Molly as she made her way into the living room.

No matter the package she came in, or how she looked, Rowan had always found her soul mate beautiful. That soul that burned brightly from her eyes and smile, and even from her skin, was unmistakable. Rowan could not help but smile again.

"Better?" Rowan asked as she came closer.

Molly nervously pulled the top of the robe tight around her and blushed as she saw Rowan's smile. "Yes, thank you," she said as she nodded her head.

"You can sit down here," Rowan offered as she motioned to the couch. "Your clothes should be dry soon. Until then, we can have some lunch and talk." She sat next to Molly on the couch, put the papers behind herself, and poured the wine for them both.

Molly took up her glass quickly and took a fortifying sip. "Rowan," she said nervously, "I guess I just need to talk to you about this morning."

"No, it's okay. You don't need to apologize," she said with a sigh. She knew it was now or never so, she chose now. "Actually, I need to talk to you about those letters you have, the ones from Lou and Jessie." She reached behind herself and put the envelope and papers back on the coffee table. "What I have to tell you," she paused, "well, I know it sounds strange but—"

"What's this?" asked Molly as she picked up the papers. "Is this what Amy was talking about? Is it what you've been working on for my screenplay?"

Rowan looked at the papers then at Molly hesitantly. "Kind of. It's their stories," she paused, "of their past lives. There have been quite a few." She watched as Molly skimmed through the pages.

"Rowan, this is…" she started and then found her words again, "this is incredible." She looked up into Rowan's face. "How did you come up with all of this so fast, so detailed?"

Rowan took a breath. She swallowed back her uncertainty. "I lived it. We lived it. I mean, they are our past lives." She hesitated at the look of confusion on Molly's face.

"What? Past lives?" Molly asked wondering where this was going.

"Okay. This is all going to sound crazy, but I need you to just hear me out." She paused for a moment and took a breath. "I'm Lou. Well, I was Lou, and you were Jessie in our past lives. Those pages are what Jessie asked me to do. It's a documentation of our lives to put with the pendant. Everything in those letters and in Jessie's journals is true. You found the pendant because you are Jessie." She ran her hand through her hair. "It's so different this time. Usually, I find it and give it to you but because of what she did, you have it."

"I don't understand," Molly said with confusion showing on her face and in her body language.

"I know," Rowan said then took a calming breath. "Those letters were written by me when I was Lou. I'm Lou." She tapped on the papers Molly was holding. "I'm Lucas and Katherine and Roger and Keith and Lou and others. You'll see when you read it all. Well, all of it isn't there because I'm still working on it. But, if you'd just look, I wrote about Lou and Jessie, too. You'll see that I know things that are in the letters and journals. You know I haven't read them all so you can compare. Then you'll believe me. I'm Lou. Louise."

"Louise? So," she frowned, "so, Lou was a woman?" Molly slowly looked through the papers feeling that the situation she was in had become surreal, and her mind was not really grasping what Rowan was telling her.

Rowan nodded slowly knowing she had probably given Molly too much information at once. "That's right, Louise was a woman and she loved Jessie very much. I loved Jessie very much. I still do." She hesitated for a moment then continued. "Molly, you are Jessie, and that's why I had to tell you this morning. I had to tell you that I love you." She watched Molly shake her head in disbelief. "I know, I know! It's crazy, but it's true! I've been doing what Jess asked by writing down everything about our past lives. I started with Jess and Lou. Please, look at what I wrote. Compare in the letters and the journals, and you'll see I know everything about them and their lives. Things that only they knew about."

Molly's panic was growing. This was crazy. What was happening to Rowan? She must have been hit harder than they thought by that rock. "Rowan. Please, don't. It isn't funny."

"I know it isn't," Rowan said, fearing that she had now ruined everything and her decision to do this now was wrong. "Listen. I know how it sounds but just read it. Oh, and look." She opened the envelope and pulled out a photograph. "Lou was a photographer. That's why she traveled so much. This is a portrait she took of herself and Jessie. See, here on the back, it's her name and Jessie's. I never thought of doing this research or documenting our lives until you showed me Jessie's letters. But now I can show you proof." Rowan looked anxiously at Molly hoping she could convince her that everything was true.

"Oh, Rowan, I..." she shook her head, "I just can't do this. I mean, past lives?"

Rowan felt that she knew the main reason Molly was hesitating and became angry with herself for making such a huge mistake. "I'm sorry. I know..." she sighed, "you're with Eric. I guess I made a mistake. Maybe this time isn't right. Maybe we just have to wait until one of us comes back as a man and the other as a woman. Maybe that's part of the curse too, that we have to be in our original forms. I don't know. Molly, I just want to be with you always. I don't care what we are, but if you can't, well, then you just can't. I'll just have to go and hope that in our next life, you can. I want you to be sure, and I want you to do what makes the person that you are now happy."

"I don't know what to say." Molly's mind reeled in confusion as she looked at the photo. "Our next life? We can't be—"

"Molly, I don't want to wait for my next life to try again. I do love you. I know it may be hard for you to understand or even believe. I know we've only known each other for a short time, but..." she looked into Molly's eyes desperately, "I don't have that much time. Since we've met, things are now in motion. Halloween is just weeks away. Please, I do love you. I love you with all of me. I love you unconditionally. Can you believe me? Can you love me, Molly? Can you, or am I making a mistake right now?" Rowan closed her eyes and resigned herself to her fate.

"Rowan," Molly said sadly and softly as she put her hand on Rowan's shoulder.

"No, it's okay," Rowan said bravely and turned away from Molly and got up from the couch and walking to the window. She looked out at the rain. It was falling even harder now. The heavens had opened up and were crying the tears that she was holding inside herself. It was over.

Molly watched Rowan as she looked out the window. She could see the pain on her face and see in her posture the sorrow that was weighing on her.

She looked at the papers and the photograph again unsure if this all could really be true. Maybe it was just Rowan trying to convince her that she loved her by making it seem as though they have a greater connection. She really was not sure.

The amazing thing was she did feel a connection to her. Even without all of these stories and the photograph, she already knew that she loved Rowan. She watched Rowan as she rubbed her temples and wiped her eyes.

Molly's heart pounded loudly in her chest, and the beat blocked the sound of the rain from her ears. She put the papers on the table, got up and walked carefully over to Rowan.

"Rowan," she said and gently touched her shoulder.

Rowan pulled away. "It's okay. I've made a mistake. I know you have your life all planned out with Eric, and it's not fair of me to do this to you now."

"Please, don't," said Molly softly. "This has nothing to do with Eric. It's me. I'm the one who has been making a mistake."

Rowan turned her head and looked at Molly. Now she was the one feeling confused.

"Rowan," Molly said and pulled her close. She raised her face to her and their lips touched gently.

Rowan closed her eyes as that familiar pull of love and desire tugged at her heart.

Molly's mind reeled at the taste and feel of Rowan. It was so comforting, and it almost seemed familiar, like something she had a long time ago as a child. "Rowan," she whispered through their kiss. "Teach me how to love you."

Rowan put her forehead to Molly's. "You know how to love me, Molly," she whispered and kissed her again.

"No," she sighed. "I mean, yes, I do love you, Rowan. I mean… I mean teach me how to make love to you."

Rowan shook her head in disbelief. "Wh—what?" Molly had just said the words she longed to hear. Suddenly, life mattered again.

Blood rushed into Molly's face and her body heated with embarrassment. "Oh, I'm sorry. I— Oh, god!" She covered her face with her hands for a moment then looked shyly up at Rowan. "I'm so sorry. It's just,"

"Molly," Rowan said as she smiled at her, "you don't have to be sorry."

"You don't understand," Molly explained as she ran her hand through Rowan's hair and her body reacted to the feel of Rowan holding her close. "All this time, I've been so confused," she stammered. "Confused about what I've been feeling, about everything, because it seemed like the only time I really felt good was when I was with you. When I left you and tried to stay away, my god, the thoughts, dreams, and pain I was feeling were overwhelming. I was supposed to love Eric, not a woman I just met. This isn't the life I thought I would lead. But I love you. I know I do. I can't deny this. I can't." She looked deep into Rowan's eyes. "I want to love you. I want to make love with you. I can't explain it. Something inside me has to be close to you, know you, all of you. Please," she whispered and kissed Rowan deeply and lovingly.

Molly followed Rowan as if she were deep inside one of her dreams to a secret place that was known by only the two of them. She was taking her to a place where no one would ever find them. In this place and time, their love was all that was inside them and all that surrounded them. It flowed out of them, one to the other and back again, bringing to the surface the truth of their emotions and desires.

Those emotions caused so many physical sensations that she knew the dream had no choice but to become the reality she ached to experience.

For that time, the world allowed them to stay in this place.

Disorientation, arousal, an aching of the heart, shortness of breath and elation, along with so many more feelings just as important, combined inside them and could only be one thing. Those combinations pushed all else aside and left only room for the consuming power of love to burn through them and sweep them away over the edge where they fell.

They fell in the love that had always meant to be for them.

Their love allowed them to bridge the distance and ride the slow turning wheel of the world as they waited for the future to welcome them into its embrace. It allowed them to share the passion, heat, and physical contact that, in Molly's dream, wasn't possible.

This love was deep, and it was felt over time and distance as they made love to each other, defying the curse that had kept them separated for so long. Their love was a portal that bypassed all obstacles that would otherwise be in the way.

Molly's desires were fulfilled in ways that her dreams could never give her, and their need for a connection with each other led to immense passion. Touching, kissing, tasting, and smelling each other's scent pushed their needs to the front, and now they were able to share themselves. Moving their bodies together reveling in the feel of skin and scent as their arousal came forth and their passion was ignited.

Lips against lips, breasts against breasts, hot center against hot center. Undulating, surging, grinding, thrusting against each other as their dripping fluids mixed with the sweat covering their bodies and filled the air with the scent of their love. Molly reveled in the feel of Rowan's touch, of her hair brushing gently against her leg as she moved her head to her center.

The light teasing probe of Rowan's tongue moving inside her caused explosions of color, strange memories, and a beautiful thrill that ran through her completely. Each movement brought need, want and desire up though each of them and into their cores and made them so sensitive that the slightest contact was all that was needed to bring them to the edge. Their sensual touches created quakes of pleasure that rocked their bodies as they were released from the exquisite pain of ecstasy.

This consummation of love bound them and gave them hope that this moment would become even more. Even though the path to their future was uncertain, the love they were feeling could sustain them. All they needed was this dream and their love and patience. All of those things they would keep in their hearts and minds along with the hope that this love would keep them together in the uncertain future.

"Molly," Rowan breathed into her ear, and Molly moaned softly in answer. "You know I love you?"

"Yes," she answered.

"You know it's all true? Everything I told you about Jessie and Lou and about us?"

Molly looked into Rowan's deep dark eyes and nodded. "I believe you. I don't know why exactly, but I do."

"You know in your soul that it's true. We're meant to be together," she whispered. "Will you do it? Will you help me? Help me stay with you so we can live this life together?"

"Yes," she answered and pulled her back to her lips to show her answer physically. Molly wanted Rowan to know without a doubt she was hers now and forever.

CHapter 18

THE DAY WAS glorious. The sky was filled with colors of pink, purple, and hues of blue after the mid-morning storm. The sun's golden rays pierced enormous fluffy clouds with arrows of light while making the pallet in the sky glow with warmth.

Molly smiled as she looked up at the sky and tried to take a deep breath. She tried to fill her lungs and body with air, but it was difficult because she was filled full with other things. She was full and overflowing with inspiration, elation, and with a devotion she had never felt for anyone before now.

She was in love.

She laughed at the tingling feeling that ran through her body from her head to her toes making a brief stop at the exact spot in her center that made her lose her breath again.

The image of Rowan, her bright smile, and sparkling eyes, floated before Molly's eyes, and she knew she was smitten, beguiled, besotted, captivated, mesmerized, and oh so very much in love.

She had been with Rowan in some way almost every day. When she was not with her, Molly's mind and her body craved Rowan. It was very difficult to think about anything else, sometimes to the point of utter distraction. She felt happier than she could ever remember feeling.

Since declaring her love for Rowan, the difference in her was extremely noticeable. Her friends had even noticed the change in her and commented on the new glow that had formed around her. They had never seen her quite so happy or laugh so much. When they asked who, what, where, and when can they meet this new person in her life who had caused such a drastic change, Molly could only smile, turn several shades of red and say, "All in good time."

Just the very thought of Rowan was putting her body and mind through such agonizing and beautiful torment this afternoon. Waking up to her touch, her kiss, and her voice was consuming her thoughts and creating an ache inside her that was deep and throbbing from her center to the edge of every nerve in her body. She was hot and flowing and tingling in anticipation of her touch. *How could Rowan make me tremble like this and be in some other place,* she wondered? She could still feel the way Rowan held her tight last night. She could still smell her and feel her making love to her all night long. She was deep inside her loving her completely.

In return, Molly loved every little part of Rowan. She was exploring and learning her, memorizing everything that makes her the wonderful person she is. It was more than physical. It was an emotional and spiritual love that she was making with her.

Rowan flowed through her body and her mind leaving traces of herself behind building memories that she would treasure always. She knew she would hold those traces dear in her heart and that they would be together forever. She knew deep inside the step she had taken in loving Rowan was the right one, and there was no doubt this was the path she wanted to follow.

The warm breeze followed Molly into the bustling restaurant. Her senses were met with the sounds of voices, the clanking of cutlery against dishes, the aroma of coffee and savory food, and the sight of colorfully dressed patrons smiling and eating their lunches. She searched through everything until her eyes focused on one person. The person she had come to meet. The person who could make her forget about everything around her. The person her body and mind craved like an addiction.

Rowan.

Molly walked straight through the crowded restaurant and made her way almost effortlessly toward Rowan.

———

"I'M SERIOUS, AMY," Rowan said as she looked intently into her unpredictable friend's eyes.

"So, what are you saying?" Amy asked with disbelief. "You think something is going to happen to you?" Her face showed just how disturbed and confused she had become.

Rowan shrugged her shoulders and set down her coffee cup. "I love her, Amy, and you're my friend. If something happens, I just want the two people I feel the closest to… I need them to help each other."

"Just because you love her doesn't mean I have to be her friend." Amy pouted.

Rowan looked at Amy wishing she could explain everything, but she knew, once she began, Amy would have a thousand questions that she would never be able to answer to her satisfaction. "Just please do this for me. No matter what she says or does, know that I need you to be her friend if something happens to me."

Amy threw up her hands in annoyance. "I don't get it. Why are you saying these things? What is she going to say or do? Why do I have to be her friend?" She saw Rowan stiffen and knew she was shutting down the conversation so she asked softly, "What's going to happen?

"I don't know," answered Rowan with a long sigh. "I just don't know. All I'm asking is that if something should happen to me, you'll help Molly," she said pleadingly. "You'll be her friend. I know how you feel about her right now."

"Oh, so now you know how I feel?" Amy blurted and crossed her arms in defiance and annoyance.

"Amy," Rowan said softly. "Please, just be her friend. Give her a chance and like I said if something should…" Rowan let her words fade as she looked up and saw Molly walking toward her through the crowd.

"What the—" Amy turned to see what Rowan was suddenly staring at with shiny eyes and her mouth open. "Oh, shit!" Amy sighed. "My new friend! Great," she said, her sarcasm thick and her eyes rolling to the side. "I just don't understand."

Rowan watched Molly approach the table entranced by the smile that she knew was just for her.

"Hi," Molly said glowingly as she leaned and kissed Rowan.

"Hi," Rowan answered then looked into Molly's eyes. She became lost in them for a moment then found her way to the soft line of her cheek then the curve of her neck. She stopped when she got to her throat. She wrinkled her brow then looked back up into Molly's eyes again.

"What?" Molly asked self-consciously.

"Where's the pendant?" Rowan asked with concern. "We need it soon. I thought you were going to wear it every day. Did you leave it at home?"

"No," Molly smiled. "It's okay. I took it to the jeweler to have it cleaned. Remember? You said it would look better if it were cleaned up. So, I took it to the jeweler you recommended. I'm going to pick it up now, and I knew you were here for lunch, so I came by to say hi." Molly kissed Rowan quickly feeling proud of herself and love for Rowan. "Wanna come?" she asked slyly with a twinkle in her eyes.

Rowan returned the smile and the memories of their time together filled her mind as she looked into Molly's eyes.

The thought of the warm night flooded her mind, and she found herself lost to the memory.

When she came in from the pool, she found Molly sleeping. She leaned gently over her and gave her some cool, wet kisses against her warm skin. Molly felt so warm and looked so beautiful as she slept. Rowan just could not resist her lips and wanted to pull her close and hold her tight. As Molly slept, Rowan sat on the lounger next to her and watched her as she dreamed. She wished she could see the images in Molly's mind.

Rowan fell asleep as the thoughts of Molly's warmth surrounded her, and she slipped into her own dream. In that dream, she could see just how Molly tilted her head when she laughed. She could see how colorful her eyes were in the sun and the dimples in her cheeks when she smiled. Rowan saw how the light rippled through Molly's hair making it dark in some places and light in others. She could feel herself memorizing Molly's features and watching her in amazement as the beauty inside and outside filled her senses.

As Rowan was lost in her presence, she heard Molly softly call her name, and she felt her kiss lightly on her lips. Oh, the taste and how it made Rowan's head swim and her body fill with desire and love for Molly. She woke slowly and felt Molly get into the lounger with her and hold her close. Molly's scent filled her and created a soothing and comfortable sensation wash over her.

"Molly, you are so beautiful." Rowan sighed. In her mind, she wanted to say so much more as Molly's hands and breath swept over her. *So lovely and graceful*, she thought. *Molly, you are in every beat of my heart, and you fill every corner of my soul*—were the words that echoed through her mind. Every word she said, every sigh she exhaled was magic. They stirred emotions deep inside Rowan that were so powerful and intense.

Rowan could feel that Molly loved deeply and fiercely. She wanted to be the one who Molly always felt that deep, fierce love for. She wanted to hold her through the nights that she needed to be held, and she wanted to love her all through the nights she needed to be loved. She hoped Molly could feel her love and how much she meant to her.

Time was getting shorter. Heartbreak was looming closer. Death was ever present. Grief for a life that may never happen was settling into Rowan's heart.

"No," she whispered sadly.

"Rowan. Are you okay?" Molly asked as she watched Rowan's troubled face. "If you can't go with me, it's okay."

"What?" asked as Rowan shook herself out of her thoughts and memories. "Oh, no. I mean yes, I can come." She looked over at Amy. "Remember what I said."

Amy crossed her arms and frowned. "Whatever," she mumbled as she watched them walk out of the restaurant.

CHapter 19

THE WALK FROM the car to the jewelry shop was warm and pleasant. The neighborhood shops were some of the few that still had their original fronts, and it felt like a step back in time as Molly and Rowan passed the heavy wooden doorways. A window display of jewel-encrusted gold and silver trinkets sparkled and greeted them as they approached.

A sharp ring from the bell triggered by the opening of the door announced their arrival to the shopkeeper. The pear shaped form of Mr. Artsvick had appeared before the old bell stopped ringing. He greeted the women with a smile and a hopeful demeanor.

"How may I help you ladies?" he asked. His eyebrows rose as he adjusted his wire frame glasses and recognized Rowan. "Ms. Cortman," he said as he stretched out his hand to her. "So nice to see you again."

"Nice to see you too, Arty," she said as she smiled charmingly and shook his hand.

"You got here very quickly," he added. "When I left you my message this morning, I thought I may have been too late."

"Message?" Rowan asked then realized what he was talking about. She had an understanding with him that if he, or if any of his colleagues, ever came across the pendant, he would let her know.

Over the years, she had purchased many art pieces from him that she found homes for in different museums. Some of the pieces were stunning and had been hidden away for years in attics and old boxes. Rowan and Arty, along with some intelligent museum curators, made it possible for the public to see the beauty and craftsmanship in the pieces.

"Yes, it just came in early this morning. I wanted you to look at it. If it's the one you're looking for, I can give your card to the young lady who dropped it off." He looked at Molly then stammered. "Oh, uh, why this," he flushed red, "this is she." He looked back and forth from one to the other. "So you've already found her? I assure you, Madame, I didn't give her your information. We pride ourselves on confidentiality and discretion. We would never..." he trailed off. His nervous stammering made Rowan smile, and Molly looked at Rowan confused.

"It's okay, Arty. I should have called you, but I didn't know the pendant would be coming to your shop today." She motioned toward Molly. "Arty, this is Molly Gentry whom you, of course, met this morning. I've known about the pendant for a few weeks." She looked at Molly and saw she was not following. "Molly, Mr. Artsvick is a friend of mine, and he's helped me find museum quality jewelry. I told him about the pendant, and I asked him to keep an eye out for it on the off chance it came into his circle."

"Yes," Arty agreed while nodding vigorously and talking quickly. "Call me Arty, please! Imagine my surprise when it actually showed up, and in one of our old boxes, at that! It was incredible! I never thought I'd see it anywhere but in the photograph. It is beautiful, just beautiful!"

"I see," Molly said softly, finally understanding why Rowan recommended this jewelry shop to her. She looked at Rowan and smiled. "So, that night when we had dinner, and you told me about your jeweler, you were making sure that if I didn't call, you would have been able to find me again if I brought the pendant here." She shook her head. "You don't miss anything, do you?"

Rowan hesitated for a moment. She did not want Molly to think she was just after the pendant. How could she think that? No, she would not think that, would she?

Molly laughed as she saw the uncertainty cross Rowan's face. "It's okay. I guess the rumor about you always getting your girl is true." She laughed.

"Uh, I guess," was all Rowan could manage.

Arty clapped his hands together with delight. "Well! Let me just get it for you now. I'll be back in just a moment," he said as he disappeared into the workroom in the back of the shop.

Rowan was not sure what to think of Molly's comment or why she even said it. She was sure she was joking but was she really? Everything with Molly had been so different this time. Molly already had the pendant and had all those letters that were written to Jessie and the journals. But that did not mean Molly was ready or understood everything at stake. It did not mean Molly trusted her or had truly felt their soul connection yet. With Jessie and many of the others, she had time. Time to get to know them, time to love them, time for them to know her completely and build a connection between them that would help break the curse.

But now, time was so short. Situations like this had never gone well in the past. How could she explain everything? Had she explained it well enough? Did Molly really understand what might happen? How could she expect Molly to trust her in just days and hours? How could she put her through all of this, the fear, the pain, and the very possible chance that Molly may witness her death?

Uncertainty was the least of what was troubling Rowan as she waited for Arty's return.

Molly watched Rowan's face as it darkened with worry. "Rowan," she said softly as she touched Rowan's arm. "What's wrong?"

Rowan looked at Molly searchingly, her eyes moving from side to side exposing her indecision. "Nothing," she answered and looked toward the back of the shop hoping that Arty would make an appearance soon.

"Something's wrong. I can feel it. I can see it on your face. Was it something I said?" Realization bloomed in Molly's mind. "It was something I said. It was what I said about you always getting your girl." She watched Rowan stiffen. "I was only teasing," she said softly and ran her hand down Rowan's arm. "I know that's not you."

Rowan closed her eyes and sighed. "How do you know that? For all you know it could be exactly who I am. We've just had so little time."

Molly pulled Rowan close, put her lips to her ear, and whispered, "It's a secret how I know," she breathed. She hesitated for a moment building suspense in Rowan. "I know that's not you because," she paused dramatically, "because Amy told me so."

Rowan let out a surprised snort of laughter. "What?"

"She did!" Molly laughed. "She told me all your secrets," Molly said in a sly secretive tone.

"Oh, really?" Rowan asked as the tension left her. She watched Molly smile back at her and was amazed at how easily she calmed her.

"Oh, yes," teased Molly. "She wanted me to be sure I knew all about you."

"Well, when did you two become so close?" Rowan asked with a chuckle, but in the back of her mind hoping that if the worst did happen, Amy would do what she asked her and truly be Molly's friend.

"Oh, days and days ago," Molly said and raised her eyebrows as she stated her fact.

"Well," Rowan said as she pulled Molly toward her. "I'm glad you two are becoming friends. What else did she tell you?"

"Sorry. Rules of friendship. I can only reveal what is said when absolutely necessary," Molly said as she felt the tingling of Rowan's breath on her lips.

"I see," Rowan said softly. Her head was spinning with desire as she moved her face closer to Molly's to taste her kiss.

"I'm so sorry!" exclaimed Arty as he appeared from the back room.

Rowan and Molly parted like guilty teenagers being caught unaware.

"You must forgive me," Arty begged.

"Why? What's happened Arty?" asked Rowan with worry.

"I am so embarrassed. It's my grandfather," Arty said expecting them to understand, but by the puzzled looks on their faces, he realized that they did not. "He insists on speaking to you. I don't understand why, but he says that he must. Do you mind?"

Rowan and Molly looked at each other, both not quite knowing what to make of the request. Rowan shrugged and looked at Arty with a wrinkled brow. "I guess we don't mind." She looked at Molly, "Do we?"

"Of course not," replied Molly as she took Rowan's hand. "Lead us to him," she said as she smiled and pulled Rowan along.

They made their way into the back of the shop past the workshop with its many jeweler tools and findings. It felt as if they had stepped back in time because the little parlor they entered looked as if it had not been redecorated since the shop was opened.

The dark antique furniture and the tidy oriental rugs covering the floor pulled the room together and made a perfect setting for the old man who lounged in the large leather chair holding onto a happily purring tabby cat. Like the old man's head, the rugs and upholstery on the furniture in the room were threadbare but spotless. The collections of knickknacks that peppered the room told the story of a long life filled with travel and adventure. The photographs that were displayed proudly showed a life of joy and companionship with family and friends, and even a few famous encounters.

"You met Louise Nevelson?" Rowan asked surprised.

"What?" The old man startled as his eyes snapped open. The cat, being disturbed by the newcomers, slowly jumped down from the old man's lap and made its way out of the parlor to another room further back in the shop.

The old man directed his attention to Rowan and the photo she was looking at and laughed. "A real piece of work, that one. Never thought she'd be so famous. Guess you can never tell."

Rowan rolled her eyes. "I guess not." She would have given her first born to have met Louise Nevelson. She had become enthralled with the sculptor's work while living in New York and regarded her as an intriguing artist.

"Who's Louise Nevelson?" asked Molly.

"Wha—" she started, "who?" Rowan asked shaking her head in disbelief. "Louise Nevelson was only one of the most important sculptors of the twentieth century." Before she could start her art history lecture, Arty interrupted.

"Grandfather, why don't you tell these ladies why you asked to see them? You did insist that I bring them to you and now," Arty hesitated, and he gestured toward the curious women, "they're here."

"I know they're here, Arty," said the elder Mr. Artsvick as he watched the two women move closer to each other. "Neither one of you looks like her," he declared.

"Who?" Molly asked as she shook her head and wrinkled her brow.

"Jessie," Rowan whispered with the shock of understanding. "You knew Jessie?"

The old man looked into Rowan's eyes and the pain that stabbed through his heart let him know immediately that she was his rival for Jessie's love. "I did," answered the old man taking a deep breath and letting it out slowly. "I'm not afraid to admit I was even a little in love with her. I didn't care that I was quite a bit younger. She was exciting and interesting, and I couldn't get enough of her. But she never looked at me as anything other than a little boy." The old man rubbed his hands over each other in agitation. "Damn it, I was more than a little in love with her. I was sure that all she was going through was a phase and just mourning for a good friend. I was sure she'd come around. She never did," he said with a short barking laugh tinged with bitterness. "The folly of youth, I guess."

Rowan looked at the old man trying to hide her annoyance, but at the same time having some sympathy for him. "It wasn't just a phase," she said with a hint of defensiveness and jealousy. This man got to spend more time with Jessie than she had. The familiar wave of pain washed over her for the many losses she held in her heart.

"No, it wasn't," Molly said softly as she touched Rowan gently on her shoulder. She could see the hurt in Rowan's face and posture. Just the knowledge that it was there inside Rowan brought Molly's emotions up through her body and threatened to push tears out of her eyes.

The old man looked up from his internal self-pity and saw the way the young blonde woman looked at the other with such transparent affection. "I know that now," he sighed. "It was something that took a long time for me to understand. Maybe I still don't understand completely. But I do know that Jessie loved Lou." The disgruntled sound in the old man's voice was evidence of his failure to get what he had wanted with Jessie.

Rowan had to move her hand over her mouth to hide the evidence of the prideful and satisfied smile that threatened to appear on her face. The old man pursed his lips and wrinkled his brow as his memories of Jessie from so long ago filled his mind.

"Her research was how we met. She was in the library, and my mother sat me down beside her. My mother didn't believe in corporal punishment like my father so her punishment was usually copy work at the library. I was copying a book that my mother thought would be good for me because of my father's business as a jeweler. Jessie had several books out on gemstones, and we started talking. She was researching the gemstone in her pendant, and before I knew it, I was helping her look up the history and myths about moonstones," he said as he shook his head. "It was because of her, I think, that I stayed in the family business." The old man shook himself out of the long ago memory and looked up with watery eyes at the two women.

"It was all strange, you know, the last few days before she died." He wheezed out a long sigh and continued. "Just a few days before she died, she had an accident in the house. That's what she said at the time, anyway. She told everyone she was repairing some wiring in the attic and was electrocuted. She said she was fine when I went to see her later."

The old man looked up at the two women expecting the shocked and concerned looks on their faces. "I believed her at the time. But now. Well, now, I just don't know. Too many strange things happened around that time."

"What strange things?" Rowan asked, her heart beating hard with concern.

The old man shrugged his rounded shoulders. "Strange things. It was the way she was obsessed with certain things like reincarnation, spirits, strange things, including the pendant you've ended up with." He furrowed his brow and scowled. "It was such a shame. She died so young. Thirty-six I think. Her heart just stopped. The coroner attributed it to her so-called accident, of course. But now, some of the things she said. I just may have to believe them."

"What? What things did she say?" Rowan asked with worry in her voice.

With a grunt, the old man shook his head. "She was very excited about something she found out about that pendant she was so obsessed with." He nodded his age spotted head at his grandson curtly.

Arty jumped to attention and handed the package with the now pristine pendant inside to Molly. He would normally take the jewelry out and place it on a piece of black velvet for the client to inspect, but he felt uncomfortable not being able to present it properly. He watched as the young woman opened the box and gently ran her finger over the piece then look over at Ms. Cortman who nodded approvingly. He felt much better seeing her approval of his work.

"When I first met Jessie," the old man continued, "all of her obsessions and strange notions seemed endearing and eccentric. But a lot of people just thought she was darn crazy. But she didn't care at all." The old man smiled. "I didn't mind either. Most people were real stick-in-the-muds back then." The old man chuckled. "We shared more than a few laughs about that."

Somberness came over the old man's expression as he continued. "She didn't seem to mind that I hung around and helped. She said she trusted me and told me I had become part of something big. I didn't really understand though at that age. Still not sure about some things. But she trusted me and she gave a direction to my life." The old man licked his dry lips and continued. "She left an envelope for anyone who found her pendant or came looking for it if I ever got hold of it. Damn strange. She said that the pendant would make its way through the world somehow and that it, or Lou, may end up in my shop someday simply because I had her letter. When I told her that my father was moving us to California, she said it didn't matter at all. She said the pendant always found its owner, and she thought the envelope would, too. Another strange thing," he said as he wrinkled his brow.

Rowan's heart was beating hard. She wanted, needed to know what this man knew about Jessie. She fought to control her impatience and felt Molly's hand run gently across her back.

After a moment of reflection, the old man continued. "But she was bound and determined that this time, the owner would be her own born again self! Can you believe that?" He gave a gruff laugh. "So she figured if her born again self was who had the pendant, Lou would be looking for it, and she wanted Lou to know some things. I moved out here not long after she passed, and I never thought the pendant would make its way here from New York so I just put the envelope away. I lived my life and had many adventures as you can see by all the photos. She was never far from my thoughts," he whispered with his rumbling voice. "Then one day, someone brought in a photo of the pendant."

He looked up accusingly at Rowan. For a long time he had been jealous of a ghost but now, after all these years, someone real was standing in front of him and the old pain flared in his chest. "I didn't say anything because I couldn't believe what she told me could really be true after all these years," he hesitated not wanting to admit the guilt he was feeling about staying silent. "Well, the pendant has made its way here, and now I have to ask myself, do I do as she asked or just forget about it and save myself from looking like a damn fool?"

"What things?" Rowan looked at Molly her mind reeling. This man had a message from Jessie—a message that had been sent through time by Jessie to Lou—to her future self. She looked at the old man and cleared her parched throat. "I hope you tell us. I know you won't seem like a fool to us if you do." She looked at Molly and gave her a nod hoping she would encourage the old man.

"Oh, no," Molly said as she fought off her confusion. "Please, tell us what she said."

Molly's thoughts were in a state of chaos. Memories of the letters she had read seemed to be part of memories that were really hers, and she felt such a strange feeling while she looked at the old man. It was almost like the familiarity she felt when she saw an old friend again after a long time, but she couldn't remember their name. There was a joy mixed with apprehension and a touch of embarrassment of her shortcoming. It stopped her in her tracks and made her feel muddled. She found it hard to speak or move. *My god*, she thought, *this must be what stage fright feels like.*

Looking up at Molly, the old man shook his head. "Well, I don't know what she said. The message is in an envelope." He looked seriously at the two women. "I'm a gentleman and gentlemen keep their word. I held on to the envelope, but I didn't open it—even though I was tempted—and I kept it safe as she asked. I was to hold onto it and then pass it and the instructions onto someone I trusted in the jewelry business if it came to it. I was planning on passing it to my grandson Arty or his daughter, of course." The old man stood up shakily on unsteady legs and walked slowly over to the bureau nearest to Rowan.

The elder Mr. Artsvick unlocked the lowest drawer with a key attached to a purple silk ribbon that had been in his pocket. Pulling out the drawer, he revealed an old gray metal lock box. He saw Rowan looking at it with wide and anticipating eyes. "Fireproof," he stated and sat it on top of the bureau. Reaching into his pocket again, he pulled out a jangling set of keys.

Rowan held her breath with anticipation for what seemed like forever as the old man found the right key, put it into the lock, then turned it and finally opened the box.

The old man gently pulled out an aged faded folder made of very thick pasteboard that had been sealed with old brown paper packing tape. It was in perfect condition. No bent corners, no creases, no markings at all. It was just faded a bit from time as old paper does.

"I'm not really sure which one of you this is meant for. She just told me it's for the one who comes looking for the pendant. I suppose that would be you," he said as he looked up at Rowan. "I didn't want to believe that someone had actually come like she said they would. I thought when you first came into the shop with that photograph it was just a coincidence. I just thought you were another collector, not..." The old man sighed and tenderly offered Rowan the folder. "I guess you're her Lou. The one she loved."

"Yes," answered Rowan softly. "I am." She swallowed and looked at Molly who was standing in silence taking in the reality of her situation. Any doubts about what the letters meant and what Rowan had told her were fading rapidly.

"I never opened it. Not in all these years," the old man reminded them while looking yearningly at the envelope. "Wanted to and was sorely tempted. But I just couldn't break the trust she had in me."

Molly put her hand on the old man's shoulder and looked kindly into his sad age-lined face. Before her eyes, his image changed, and she could see him as he was when she was Jessie. She smiled and saw his eyes widen as recognition came to him. She kissed him on his stubbled cheek. "Thank you. Thank you for helping us."

The old man's eyes began to water, and he nodded bravely. "It really is her," he said in astonishment.

Chapter 20

THE DRIVE TO Rowan's office was filled with a thick silence. Anticipation, wonder, fear, uncertainty, and curiosity were only a few of the emotions that were being felt by both women, but neither dared to break the silent contemplation of the other.

Between them lay what may be the answers to the rest of their lives together. It could be the answers they needed to break the curse. Or it may only be a message of love and encouragement from the past. In the worst case, a letter confirming this curse had no end, and they would be doomed never to have a life together.

Molly parked the car and looked at Rowan.

They could see the apprehension in each other's eyes.

Rowan sighed and opened the envelope. She pulled out the letter from the past and read it aloud.

My Dearest Lou,

How I desperately hope that you are reading this finally.

If you are, it means we will be together again soon, or my highest hope, that we are together at the very moment you are reading this message.

Since I can't be sure of your circumstances, I must begin from your end.

How heartbreaking and terrible it was for me to lose you.

Even now it is too heartbreaking for me to describe that reality on paper. I admit that, for some time, I was truly lost without you. It may be no surprise to you that my recovery came when a lawyer showed up at my door with your will and the last letter you wrote to me.

It's funny to me now what I noticed then. It was that you said nothing about the curse in your letter, but instead, only reassured me, one last time, that our love and time was not truly over but only delayed. After reading your letter over and over again and crying for what seemed like days, it came to me like a gift from you.

In that moment of clarity came an epiphany that burned into my very core.

I must find you again no matter the cost.

My quest became finding a way to break the curse and bring us together again. In essence, your quest, throughout all of your many lives became mine. But I only had this single lifetime, so I knew I must go to some great extremes.

I left messages to my future self and to you, but I did not include some very important things. I kept these things hidden for a single reason—to know them is to be in great danger.

I need you to know that by writing this, I am in danger, and I am putting you and my future self in danger. At this moment, I am protected only by a small window of time, but I know when it ends, my life will be short. I have been battling those forces that hold the curse over us since shortly after I began my quest. I know I cannot defeat them alone now.

To break the curse, we must be together again.

With this knowledge in mind, I must ask you to stop here if you have not found me or if the time for the ceremony is a long time off. Seal this back in the envelope, keep it safe, and don't look at it again until it is time.

Once you read past this page, I fear that forces will begin to try to harm you and make it so that you cannot carry out the process of breaking the curse. Their strength in this world has been our weakness, and once we break the curse, they know that they will lose their hold here. Over the years, they have lost the fact that this curse was supposed to be a gift. It was a fickle gift of a bored spirit, however. Now the gift has become something they don't want us to have, and they have been working hard to keep us in this cursed state.

The only protection I can give you is this warning. After the seal is broken, you will be revealed, and the forces WILL come.

My darling, I am here now, and I know that I will be there waiting for you somewhere when you are back in this world. All I can do now is give you this last gift from another lifetime.

Always and forever,

Jessie

ROWAN FINISHED READING the letter inside Molly's car. She turned it over then back again. She looked in the old folder again. Then she looked inside the perfectly preserved manila envelope that the letter came out of again. She looked up at Molly. "Where's the rest?"

Chapter 21

THE EARLY MORNING sun shone in on Molly's neatly organized desk. She had promised Rowan that she would leave as early as possible today. Today was the day. It was the day that had been hanging so heavily over them since they got the letter from Jessie.

She looked at the letter on her desk, ran her hands through her hair in frustration, and then sighed heavily.

"What are we missing?" she asked under her breath. She looked down at the letter again. It was a letter from another lifetime that was a part of her soul, and probably the most important part of her future.

It was difficult for her to get a handle on the concept. She was the author of the letter, well, in another life, in another time. So if she wrote the letter, why had she not just 'known' what was in it? Why did Rowan get to remember everything and she was without a single memory? It didn't seem fair.

The reason she had the letter at this very moment was simply because she 'wrote' it and it was possible that she would be able to figure out what she, as Jessie, did to hide the message meant for them now. They had to figure this out before the ceremony Rowan said they had to perform. That ceremony was tonight.

Molly looked closely at the letter again. The ivory paper was thick and of good quality. It looked very expensive. The border was edged with a gold line at the top and down the left-hand side. The lines stopped just before the script letter 'J' that was embossed in the upper left corner. Simple and elegant. The handwriting was clear and in neat cursive that was easy to read. There were no odd inkblots or unusual punctuation. There were no creases or folds because it was placed flat in the envelope.

Molly picked up the envelope and looked inside again. She turned it over and examined it for the possibility of a hidden pocket. Nothing. She threw it back on her desk in frustration. "Where the hell is the rest?" she exclaimed for the thousandth time.

A sharp knock on her door announced the sudden appearance of Terry from accounting. "Molly, emergency meeting in conference room B! We all have to be there now! Come on!"

"Shit!" hissed Molly as she jumped up from her chair. She shoved Jessie's letter and her meeting files into her case, grabbed her purse, and followed Terry out the door.

———————

IT FELT LIKE nothing had gone right today for Molly. She got a riddle from the past that she could not figure out. The so-called emergency meeting was a disaster, and now she was running late to meet Rowan.

"Good grief." She sighed as she made it to her car. She could not believe how bad the meeting was. At first, it seemed like things were going to be resolved quickly, and she could get back to her office to have time to look at the letter again, but then there was a sudden shift, and no progress was made at all. It seemed as if one little comment opened a can of worms and they could not be shoved back into the can.

Molly always felt most of the meetings she had to sit in on were unproductive and a waste of her time, but this one was an absolute travesty. The executive who called the meeting was unorganized, and it seemed he had no idea what was going on with the production process. Budget concerns turned into studio issues that turned into talent issues that then led to personal attacks that placed blame and wasted time. She could not wait until she had enough experience to become a production executive so she could call the meetings and actually get things done.

Right now, though, she was having doubts about her career in the movie industry. After today, she didn't know how she felt about telling anyone about her relationship with Rowan. Her head swam with worry. She saw how it could be used against her, and frankly, it was scary. Would her relationship with Rowan ruin her career? She shook her head. She could not understand why those thoughts were filling her mind. She knew several gay people who were in the business. They were all men, but still, men always seem to have it easier no matter what. No, that's not true. How could she think that?

This industry was based on talent and creativity, in addition to money. Surely, sexual orientation for men or women could not play into things. Molly sighed. She knew it could and did at times. She had seen it. Would she be able to get ahead or would she be overlooked because she was in a relationship with a woman?

"Oh, God!" she shouted in frustration. "What the hell am I doing?" She fumbled in her purse for her keys.

"Molly!" An all too familiar voice shouted at her. "I've been looking for you."

Molly looked around and groaned. *Not now*, she thought. "Eric, what are you doing here?"

"You know I've been trying to talk with you."

"I have nothing to say to you."

"Molly, please," Eric said softly as he grabbed her arm.

"Let go of me!" she said as she tried to pull away. She felt his grip tighten around her arm. "I said let go!"

As Molly wrenched her arm away, the violence of the motion slung her purse and briefcase out of her hand and onto the ground. Both leather containers burst and spilled their contents over the pavement.

"Damn it!" she shouted in anger. "I just don't have time for this!" She attempted to retrieve the things from her purse and tried to get her papers back into the case as quickly as possible.

Eric watched her struggle but did not lend a hand. He looked at Molly and his anger at her increased. "What are you doing? I mean, my god!" he exclaimed with frustration. "You can't really be going out with that, that woman!" He watched as Molly did her best to ignore him and continued. "Think of your career, your future, us! You can't really think that she's better than me! That's just crazy! You're not even a real lesbian for god's sake!"

Molly looked up as she pressed her briefcase closed even though papers still protruded out from the sides. She could see by Eric's ruddy complexion that he was coming to a boiling point. Just under the calm he tried to portray, he was ready to explode at any moment. That knowledge could not stop her sharp words.

"You have no idea what I am or what I'm not. You never have, and you've never really cared! Just go away and leave me alone!"

"Molly, come on. Listen to reason. I know you want a family and a home. Who's going to be the father of your children? Or now suddenly are you going to be content to have no children? I know you want them. We talked about it."

By the look on Molly's face, he could tell he had hit on something that was close to her. The uncertainty he saw in her face registered in his mind as a weakness, and he jumped on the opportunity. "With her, you'd have nothing," he whispered. "Absolutely nothing. No family, no children, no career—no future at all. Molly, you don't even really know what it means to be a lesbian. As soon as people find out, you will lose everything."

"Shut up!" she cried, and tears began to run down her face. Eric's words tore her. Questions filled her mind, and it felt like her head was about to explode.

What would happen to her dreams and desires? Would she really have to give up everything she wanted to be with Rowan? She had never felt the way she felt over the last few weeks with anyone, not even Eric. She looked at him standing in front of her. His perfect suit and hair, that stupid superior look and clenched fists. Why was he doing this? He never really loved her. Oh, he cared for her, thought she would make a good wife and mother, but there was always that feeling she was just an accessory and not a real part of his life. He just expected her to be there when he called.

She couldn't believe all this time she had lived like that with him. She didn't care about him either, though. He was just as convenient for her. She had her career and someone to take to parties. She had someone who fit the picture in her mind of what a family should be like with a mother, father, and children. Was that all she wanted? Should she hope for more? Would it be the same with Rowan or would it be different? She had not even known Rowan long enough to have a conversation about children.

Oh, my god, she thought, *I have no idea what it means to be a lesbian.* "What the hell am I doing?" she asked herself under her breath. Her body began to shake as every doubt that Eric verbalized ran through her mind over and over again. They were the very doubts she had before about her relationship with Rowan.

Eric's anger turned into a condescending sympathy. "It's okay, Molly. A lot of people experiment," he paused, "are curious," he nodded, "and that's all this is. It won't last, and I think you know it. I mean," he gave a nervous laugh, "how can it, really?" Eric hesitated, and Molly's non-responsiveness encouraged him to go on. "Maybe I pushed you too hard about your screenplay. I understand now how important your career is to you. We can work things out. Maybe now we can finally get married. Make it official. Lots of women work and have children. Just come back to me and you'll see. This thing with Rowan," he tried to reason, "it's just something you couldn't help. She does this sort of thing all the time. She isn't for you. Her lifestyle isn't yours. I'm the one, Molly. I'm the one for you. Please, say you'll stop all of this and come back to me." He looked into her wide and searching eyes trying to think of anything else he could say to convince her. She looked away from him, and he blurted out in a panic. "Come on! You can finish the damn script you're working on, and when that's done, then we can get married."

Molly snapped her head up and looked back into Eric's face. "What? My script?" She put her hand to her head as she wavered and her knees weakened. She closed her eyes to help stop her head from spinning. The letters from Jessie to Lou. That love. That life. That is what she wanted more than anything. She realized she could never have that with Eric. Maybe she could find it with Rowan. Maybe. "I..." She took a step back. "I have to go."

She opened her car door and threw her purse and briefcase into the passenger seat. The case fell to the floor of the car and broke open again. "Shit!" She got in the car and tried moving the papers back into the case. "I have to go, Eric. I have to go see Rowan. She's waiting for me."

"No, she's not." he said and crossed his arms.

"What?" she said as she shook her head in confusion.

"She's not. I left a message on her answering machine. I told her you were coming back to me and going back to your normal life." He smiled and nodded his head.

"How…" she sputtered in disbelief, "how could you?"

"Now you don't have to go see her. You're free. You can come back to me now," he explained, not understanding how she could not see the huge favor he had done her.

"Eric. I…" She hesitated. She looked down at the mess in her briefcase. She looked at the letter from Jessie lying in the seat. *That was strange*, she thought as she looked at it. She picked it up and looked closely at it. The paper was bent and splitting in the upper left-hand corner near the embossed 'J.' She put her finger on the top layer and pulled it away from the bottom slowly and carefully.

"Molly!" shouted Eric at the top of his lungs and slapped the letter out of her hands. "Come on! I told you that you don't have to go. You need to come with me!"

Eric's sudden movement left Molly in shock. She felt him grab her arm and begin to pull her out of the car, but the image of the letter was still filling her mind.

The rest of the message was there.

She tried to pull away from Eric, and she lost her sense of real time. It seemed like a dream. She moved toward Eric as he pulled on her, and then, with a sudden jerk, she pulled away and somehow got her feet into the car. She pulled on the door as Eric recovered and grabbed for it. His face was in a full rage, and as the car door closed, he beat his fists on the window.

Molly could hear Eric bellowing outside the car as she locked the doors. She fumbled in her purse for her keys and got them into the ignition.

She turned the key.

It wouldn't start.

The damn car would not start. Her heart was thundering in her chest. Eric's ranting assault on the car was a low undercurrent of sound. Her mind was spinning out of control. She turned the key again.

The engine came alive, and the cool air from the air conditioner blew into her hot and flushed face. She put the car into gear and stepped on the gas, leaving Eric behind as he yelled and waved his fists.

"Oh, my god. Oh, my god. Oh, my god!" Molly spilled out. Her body was shaking, and her grip on the steering wheel was white-knuckle tight. She looked over at the letter that had landed on the passenger floorboard. She could see the corner that had begun to separate further. She took a deep breath and tried to calm herself.

Her hand shook as she reached down for the letter. It was just out of her reach. A car horn blared; she jerked the steering wheel and stepped on the breaks. "Fuck!" she screamed as tremors of fright ran through her body at the near miss. She took a calming breath and looked in the passenger seat at her cellular phone. She picked it up and dialed. She listened impatiently as it connected and went to voicemail. "Rowan! Rowan, I'm coming!" she shouted desperately. "Rowan, I found out where the rest of the message is! I'll be there as fast as I can!"

Chapter 22

TWELVE FACES CONFRONTED the October breeze, each one lonely in its watch that would last deep into the night. They awaited a ritual that had spanned many lifetimes. Their creator set them gently into place and now looked over them with satisfaction and knowledge that they were alert and watchful. Sadness enveloped the scene and was carried by the wind over the many faces. As the wind blew through the faces, they could feel the despair and hopelessness it carried. It brought out a low moan from each of them in response.

Rowan looked over her work—work she had done alone, again. *How many times had she had to do this alone?* she thought. Too many. Her vision blurred as tears of hopelessness filled her eyes. She did not allow them to fall. She could not. She blinked the tears away and stood firm. The twelve pumpkins were in place. She would wait a while before she lit the candles and spoke the spells. No need to rush now. She would do the ritual as she had always done, even though there was no need to do anything really.

Molly wasn't coming.

Walking back inside the house, Rowan carried in the last pumpkin—the one to hold her heart—to the hearth, setting it down gently. She wondered, for the thousandth time in this life, what would happen if she didn't set out this pumpkin. Would everything stop? She was getting so tired of never succeeding, tired of hoping and trying so hard all the time and never getting any closer to the end. She was tired of making plans and dreaming of a future that never came. She really thought, this time, it would be different. What Jessie had done was amazing. She had given hope where there was uncertainty, but even that hope was not enough.

Rowan was not really surprised that Molly had changed her mind. It had happened before. Everything this time, though, had happened so suddenly. Things got really scary really fast, and she could understand why Molly decided she couldn't go through with it. She tried calling her after she got the message from Eric but kept getting voicemail.

She wondered if Molly really thought she was crazy like Eric said in his message. Everything did sound a bit crazy—the letters Molly found, the pendant, everything they had learned from Jessie, and what she had told Molly—all of it, crazy.

Rowan looked at the stack of pages on her desk. She finally finished. She had documented everything. She left a copy for Molly and a copy in a place she may get access to in the future if she returned and remembered again. Right now, she didn't feel like she wanted to return. Not that she had much of a choice. If she could choose, though—no, she couldn't think this way. There had to be a way to break the curse. It was just, her heart hurt so much right now she could hardly stand it.

The memories of all her lives flowed through her mind. The knowledge of each one ending in disappointment and heartache overwhelmed her, and her body shook with sorrow. Now it had to happen again. As she looked at the pendant that had found her so many times, she remembered the love she felt when she was Lucas, so long ago. She moved her fingers across the stone and remembered the day she gave it to Evelyn. She remembered the love for Evelyn, who first had the soul that Molly had now.

"What a fucking waste of time!" Rowan cried and gripped the pendant tightly in her hand.

She looked down at the stack of paper, the story of her lives, with tears finally breaking away, streaming from her eyes and soul. All those years, months, days. So many. Too many to count. Too many too painful to remember. Every chance of a lifetime with her soul mate cut short by this damn curse. With a shuddering sigh of resignation, Rowan put the pendant in her pocket and turned away from the pages filled with her past.

Though in her future, she saw nothing but darkness, she followed through with her preparations for the ceremony. It was her tradition that every Halloween, she performed the ceremony. She performed it to keep the smallest hope that might be inside her alive, even when she was unable to feel that hope at all. While she worked checking each small bottle of powder, trimmed candlewicks, and cleared a space for the ceremony, she let her mind slip into old memories.

The days that were spent with Evelyn so long ago seemed like yesterday. She gave a short laugh at the thought of how people today believe time long ago was easier. Love is hard no matter when you are born.

Molly's decision not to come shouldn't be surprising, Rowan thought. She recalled her own difficulty when she was Roger, and she had found Mark. It was the first time they had both been the same sex. It was hard on both of them to get past the fact that they were both men. Especially Mark. When they were close, it was hard to breathe, and the confusion inside them brought them both to tears.

When they were together, it was like melting into bliss. They were meant to be together. Just like she and Molly belonged together now.

Molly.

Her face blended with all the faces Rowan had seen her soul possess. She was the same in every one of them. She was the one she would love forever.

Rowan shook her head to clear the fog of memories. She understood what Molly was going through. It was just too bad they didn't have more time together. If they did, maybe things would be different. She would have time to talk with her, walk with her in the sun, dance with her in the rain, cry with her, fight and make up with her and make love with her again. But time was not always a friend. There was either too little or too much depending on when or if she found her love.

Wiping her hands on her jeans, she took stock of all her work. Everything was ready. The only thing missing was Molly. She looked out the window at the carved faces guarding the house. There would be no need to light the candles tonight. No need to prolong the inevitable. She turned away and went to the couch where she laid down and pulled the pendant from her pocket. She stared into it and let the moonstone fill her vision. She wondered if Molly would come back for it after she died. They had decided to keep it safe at the house after picking it up from the jeweler. Molly seemed nervous about wearing it after learning how valuable it was and how important it was for breaking the curse. She insisted that keeping it safe in one place felt like the right thing to do. Rowan decided she would put it inside the envelope for Molly to make sure she got it back.

Rowan felt so tired. Maybe if she went to sleep and didn't wake up in time, she could miss it all and wake up in another life. No, she could not sleep long. She had to be up in time to see if she could gain any more knowledge, any new clue to breaking the curse. She would face the demons again. She would face them alone. She gripped the pendant tightly as she made up her mind that she would face them for as long as it took, but right now, her heart was hurting. She needed to sleep. She would have to be ready for tonight.

As Rowan drifted away, a cold breeze swept through the house. They were here now surrounding her.

The phone rang, but the spirits muffled the sound of Molly calling.

———————

HER EYES WIDE and her teeth set hard together, Molly's breath came in quick heaving gasps of desperation. Jessie's letter was held tightly in her hand. Molly tried to keep the seal from breaking open anymore by squeezing the separating corners closed.

She quickly determined earlier that 'it' was the cause of her situation. 'It' was the cause of this danger, yet she had to keep 'it' with her because it also held the answers they needed. "Oh god, Rowan. Please, be okay. Oh god, please let me make it to her," she whimpered.

She saw now why all of this was happening to her today. It was all because of the letter. She also knew this was only the beginning, and it was only going to get worse.

No, this was not the beginning. The beginning was when she shoved the letter into her case while in her office. She must have bent the corner and partially broken the seal then. That was why the meeting went the way it did. That was why Eric came. When she dropped her case, the seal opened even more. That was why this was happening to her now.

She could feel the heat of the invisible forces that were with her in the car. She tried desperately to escape, but the doors wouldn't open, and the windows wouldn't budge. She fought the steering wheel desperately with all of her might to keep the car on the road.

Tears of fear ran down her face, and with every stinging contact, the spirits surrounding her brought cries of pain from her lips.

"Please," she cried. "Please, stop it!"

The buttons in the car were pressed or turned by the malevolent force. The car was hot from the heater, and she fought to get cool air so that she could breathe.

A sharp cracking sound made her look up suddenly from her fight with the steering wheel. She watched helplessly as a line was formed in her windshield. There was a loud crack, and she reacted instinctively, turning her head and closing her eyes as, suddenly, there were a thousand minute cracks and the safety glass exploded. Tiny pieces of glass flew over her.

"Fuck!" she screamed as she slammed on the breaks.

She flew forward and up, hitting her head on the ceiling of the car. The stinging pain from the impact moved down her head and to the bridge of her nose making it hard for her to take a breath. The air from outside was a relief, but she had no time to notice. She gripped the steering wheel and the letter tighter as more tears ran down her face. She let out a scream of defiance and put her foot down hard on the gas. She had to make it to Rowan.

———————

THE WORLD HAD melted into wonderland.

Rowan looked around her, and she wasn't sure how she got there because she couldn't remember seeing a white rabbit. She stumbled down the path least followed and found Molly debating upon which mushroom would be most suitable for her situation.

"Molly," she exclaimed, "I'm so glad I found you! You know this path is so uncertain."

Molly looked at Rowan and nodded her head with a furrowed brow. "I know. It's a scary path to follow."

Rowan watched as Molly dropped the pieces of mushroom she held and brushed her hands off on her purple skirt. "Well," she declared, "since you're here, I don't have to eat that mushroom. We can follow the path together, and it won't be as scary."

Rowan nodded in agreement. "Okay, I think you're right. We can do it together."

They found their way down the path and came to a shabby but interesting looking hut surrounded by a colorful garden full of butterflies.

"Oh, aren't they beautiful!" Molly exclaimed.

Rowan smiled as she watched Molly look at them in wonder. "Look at those flowers," she whispered in amazement. "Let's go smell them. They are so beautiful."

They made their way to the flowerbed. As they approached, a little man in an opera hat that was lower on one side than the other came out of the crooked hut. "Stop right there!" he demanded in a squeaky voice. "I say, you should back away, ladies, if you know what's good for you."

The women looked at each other and then back at the little man. "How rude! We were just going to admire these flowers," Molly tried to explain. "So if you don't mind, sir, we'll continue!"

"Yes, I can almost smell them from here. We have to go closer," Rowan said to the little man.

He stared at them for a moment and looked them up and down, then began to speak but was cut off by a shrill voice behind him that made him cringe and hunch his shoulders.

"Jus' wha' do ya thin' you're doin'? I tol' ya ta bring in the kettle!" shrieked a small woman clothed in several layers of scarves and lace, and on her head was a bonnet hosting a small yellow bird.

"I'm keeping these women from trampling our flowers. I'll bring the kettle in a bit," the little man complained.

"Hey!" Rowan exclaimed. "We weren't going to trample them. Just smell them!"

The old woman stuck her nose into the situation and looked them over even closer than the old man had.

As the old woman looked them over, Rowan whispered softly to Molly, "Now we know why it's the path least followed."

Molly laughed and hugged Rowan tight, and then she rewarded her with a kiss for making her laugh. "I think I'm falling for you!" she declared, and Rowan smiled from her heart.

The old woman demanded their attention again. So being the very polite people they were, Rowan and Molly turned to listen.

"So, ya wan' ta smell me flow'rs, do ya?" she asked. They both nodded, and she continued, "Okay," she shrugged, "I jus' 'ope ya know wha' you're gettin' yer selves inta."

They looked at each other and rolled their eyes at her crazy comment. "Come on," Rowan said as she pulled Molly to the flowerbed.

They stepped up to the edge of the bed. The flowers were large and purple with white lines from the base to the tip of the petals. They leaned forward and inhaled their scent. It was amazing, remarkable, and incredible!

Rowan and Molly were filled with the scent of the flowers, and without warning, the strange world they had found began to slip away. They looked at each other and felt a stirring inside, a pull that was irresistible. Suddenly, they could see what was not there before, and joy overtook them.

They frolicked through the garden and came upon a wondrous sight. It was a seven foot round bed surrounded by sweet smelling flowers and fragrant fruit trees. As they looked in wonder at the sight, a cloud covered the sun and swathed the garden in a romantic darkness.

Rowan looked at Molly, desire burning in her, and she touched Molly's shoulder. "I want to make love to you, here in that round bed, in this beautiful garden."

Molly looked into Rowan's eyes, and all reason left them both as they made their way to the bed and climbed up into it.

Rowan kissed Molly gently as she removed her clothes, throwing them aside with abandon. She ran her hands over Molly's body and moved her kisses to her breasts as she pushed her back on the bed. The dream filled with images that made their minds spin and their hearts race. Two bodies entwined. Lips open and waiting with anticipation. Rowan looked into hazel eyes that were inviting and filled with desire. In this dream, the time and distance between them were nonexistent.

They softly touched.

They tenderly kissed.

Suddenly, a hot tearing sensation ran down Rowan's back, and she screamed out in pain. She tried to flip around to see what was happening, but a force was holding her down.

"This is not to be!" boomed a laughing voice. "This will never be real! We are here now. Come along. It is time for dreams to end, and your life to begin again."

"No!" Rowan shrieked as she fought the force holding her down and broke away so that she could see where the familiar voice was coming from. "No, it isn't time! You've come too early!"

A smoky form appeared before them, and it shrugged with an evil grin. "We are here now." The demon looked at Molly and waved its hand through the air. "Be gone."

"No, no, no!" Rowan screamed as she tried to hold onto Molly, but she fell away like sand and was carried away by the wind. "No!" Rowan cried out again. But this time, her cry was filled with rage and pain. "Molly! Molly! No! Come back!"

The booming voice pealed with laughter at the sight of Rowan in turmoil. "Remember, she doesn't want to come back. She doesn't love you. She will never truly love you. Can't you see that after all these years?"

The demon's words echoed in Rowan's mind. She covered her ears and fell to her knees in despair.

"Molly," she whispered through her tears. She called for her to come back over and over again while trying to block out the demon's mocking laughter that surrounded her.

Chapter 23

THE AIR WAS black and toxic. Smoke filled the air and blocked out all that was bright—the sun, the white clouds, and the world. It filled the world with a rancid stench that only a demon would favor.

Hell had come to earth.

The damaged and smoking car came to a halt at the end of the driveway. Coughing and with eyes watering, Molly threw the door open. She leaped from the car with only Jessie's letter in her hand and stumbled as she ran frantically toward the doorway.

Breathing hard, she could not help but look behind her for the forces she could not see. She ran to the steps and hurdled up them, making it onto the porch in a single motion. She reached for the door handle and tried desperately to turn it without success. She pulled on the handle and pounded on the door.

"Rowan!" she shrieked. "Rowan, open the door! Rowan, it's Molly! Hurry! Please! Rowan!" She ran to the living room window and peered inside for Rowan. The curtains blocked her view, so she pounded her fist on the window making the panes rattle. "Rowan! Where are you? Rowan!" She looked back at the car and knew there was no way she was getting back inside.

She had to get into the house.

Molly made her way to the back of the house. The sliding glass door was closed, and the curtains were drawn. "Damn!" She knocked on the door and called out, but there was still no answer. "Oh, god. What am I going to do?" she asked herself anxiously. She leaned against the door and put her face close so that she could get a good angle to see between the curtains. She moved up and down to find the right height and angle to see inside. She stopped. She saw the couch and thought she saw something move. *No—someone.*

She saw Rowan lying on the couch, and her heart raced.

"Rowan!" she cried with renewed hope, but Rowan didn't move again. She looked down at Jessie's letter and the image of her damaged car and what she went through flashed in her mind's eye. Fear struck Molly to the core. "No! Rowan! Rowan! Wake up! Oh, god, please let her just be asleep. Don't let them be here. Rowan!"

Rowan didn't wake up.

Running as fast as she could back to the front of the house, Molly flew onto the porch. She made her way over to the living room window and tried desperately to look inside. She looked around and ran her hands through her hair, not knowing what to do. She stopped and looked down at the porch then back at the window.

"I hope you can forgive me, Rowan," she said and bent down to take off her high-heeled black leather shoe. She held the toe of the shoe in her hand and swung the stylish heel with all of her might into the windowpane. With just a few strikes, the glass cracked then shattered. She used the shoe to clear the broken glass.

"Fuck! I loved these shoes!" She reached her hand inside and unlocked the latch. The window opened easily as she pushed it up. She looked inside and called out. "Rowan? Rowan, I'm coming in."

She climbed carefully through the window avoiding the broken glass as best she could. Slipping off her other shoe, Molly took a step forward, and suddenly, she could feel that the air inside the house was thick. The hairs on the back of her neck stood on end, and she swallowed back her fear. She rushed to the couch where Rowan was lying very still. She knelt next to her and gently touched Rowan's face.

"Rowan?"

Rowan's pale face was warm, and her hair was curled and damp from perspiration. Her body was rigid, and her fists were clenched tight. Molly could see slight tremors as Rowan's eyes moved under her eyelids and a tear streamed out. She was dreaming. Molly gently nudged Rowan's shoulder hoping to wake her without startling her.

"Rowan," she whispered anxiously into her ear. "Rowan, wake up. Please, wake up. They're coming." Nothing. Rowan was non-responsive. "Fuck! Fuck! Fuck! Fuck!" Molly said quickly under her breath.

She ran to the kitchen and slid to the sink where she grabbed a dishtowel and ran it under some cool water from the sink and then wrung it out. Rushing back to the couch, she could hear Rowan's voice calling her. "I'm here! Rowan, I'm here." She leaned over her and wiped Rowan's forehead with the cool towel. "Oh, please. Please, wake up."

Molly stood up and looked around the room. She could see that Rowan had everything ready for the ceremony just as they had planned. She looked back at Rowan and knew she had no choice. She could see that something was wrong with her, and she had to wake her up. She had to do it now before whatever was in the car came in and joined whatever might already be in the house. The sound of Rowan's moan brought Molly back into the present, and she sat beside her on the couch. Molly blotted the perspiration from Rowan's face.

"Rowan, I need you to wake up right now." She put the towel aside and leaned over Rowan putting her arms under Rowan's and then around her body. She pulled her up into a sitting position. "Come on, Rowan. Wake up!" she whispered quickly into her ear.

"No!" growled Rowan as she thrust her arms out to free herself from the demons in her dream.

Rowan's sudden outburst sent Molly reeling back. "Fuck!" she cried as she landed hard on the floor. Molly looked up at Rowan and saw her looking around in confusion. "Damn! You're hard to wake up!"

Rowan looked down at Molly who was holding herself up in a half-sitting position. *She is missing her shoes,* Rowan thought in her confusion. Then she blinked and realized she was back in her own home. She was back, and Molly was here. "Molly?" she asked to make sure she was real.

"Yeah," Molly confirmed. "Thanks for knocking me on my ass," she quipped as she got to her knees.

"Sorry," was all Rowan could manage as she tried to get her mind focused back into reality.

Molly knelt in front of Rowan and looked into her eyes. She could see Rowan was still confused and not totally with her yet. She took Rowan's face in her hands and made Rowan look at her.

"Rowan, you have to snap out of it." She looked over her shoulder at the front door and then back at Rowan. "Rowan, they're here. I found Jessie's hidden message and broke the seal. Now they're here, and we have to do something!"

"You broke? You broke the seal?" Rowan watched as Molly nodded her head with fear in her eyes. Realization of what Molly was saying burned away the fog in Rowan's mind. She pulled Molly to her feet. "The candles! We have to light the candles!" She pulled Molly with her as she ran out the door to get to the circle of pumpkins that surrounded the house.

With nervous haste, Rowan and Molly lit the candles and recited the spell that they had said so many times in different lives. "Come power to protect, to fight and to unite." They repeated it each time they lit a candle inside a grim-faced pumpkin. "Come power to protect, to fight and to unite."

As they repeated the spell, they could feel the forces surround them. They could feel them trying to prevent them from lighting each candle. But they fought on united until all of the candles were lit. They fell back on the ground exhausted and covered in perspiration.

For the first time, Rowan looked intently at Molly as she lay breathing hard beside her and tears threatened to fill her eyes.

She came back, she thought. *She came back.*

———————

THOUGH THEY WERE safe for the moment, both knew their time was running out. The ring of pumpkins and the spell should hold the demons back at least until the sun went down. At the dining room table, Rowan and Molly looked at Jessie's final letter, and at the corner having separated, breaking the seal. They looked up at the same time and into each other's eyes. They both knew they had to break the rest of the seal to read the message left for them. They both knew this might be the last moment they had together that would be relatively safe. As soon as the seal was fully broken, there was no telling what might happen. If they opened it now, they might have time to figure things out. If they wait, it may be too late to do anything Jessie might tell them to do.

"I think we should wait," said Molly shakily.

"Wait? Why? That may not be a good idea," Rowan replied with worry.

Molly shrugged her shoulders blinking back tears. "We know that things outside will get worse when we break the seal. I want…" She looked away from Rowan shyly.

Rowan could see Molly was trying not to cry. "What? What do you want?" she whispered.

Molly took a deep calming breath. "I know it may sound weird or crazy. I just…" She looked into Rowan's waiting eyes and her words tumbled out. "So much has happened. I've been so scared. I feel like I've been so far away from you. I'm scared that if everything is true and if this doesn't work—" She nodded toward the paper on the table then looked back at Rowan. "I'll never get to, to be close to you again. If I lose you now—" She covered her face with her hands to hide the tears that she could feel were coming. "Oh, god. This is so fucked up!" she said in a muffled cry. "I don't know what I'm saying!"

Rowan watched Molly and could see the pain and longing in her. "I know what you're saying. It's okay." She stood and took Molly's hand and pulled her up from her chair. She moved in close and kissed her sweetly and gently.

"You know?" Molly asked softly as a tear fell down her face.

"Yes," answered Rowan, and she kissed her tear away and pulled her close into a warm embrace. She held Molly and felt her sigh and shake, as she cried. Her own tears weren't far behind, but she held them back. This was always the hardest moment when it came.

Saying goodbye.

She lifted Molly's head up and kissed her again. "I want to be close to you, too. It's okay. Come on."

She led Molly into the bedroom, and they sat on the bed. Molly put her arms around Rowan and pushed her back onto the bed and kissed her. She sat up and looked at Rowan who was watching her with those eyes so full of love and sorrow. Molly unbuttoned her blouse and took it off exposing her breasts for Rowan. She moved over Rowan and pressed her body against her.

She wanted to be so close to her.

Skin close.

Soul close.

The desire to taste every part of Molly overtook Rowan. As Molly kissed her deeply, Rowan rolled herself overtaking Molly with her. She began methodically kissing and tasting Molly's body. She licked and kissed her neck and ears, and then ran her tongue down her neck to the place where her neck and shoulder met. She twirled her tongue there breathing her hot breath onto Molly. She felt Molly arch at the sensation as a moan left her lips.

Molly ran her hands through Rowan's hair as Rowan reached under her and unclasped her bra. Rowan traveled down Molly's body to her chest then to her breasts. She pushed her bra up and took Molly's breast into her mouth running her tongue around her nipple and sucking it gently. Rowan was creating a need inside Molly that had to be satisfied.

Molly pulled Rowan back up, kissing her and tugging at her shirt. She wanted to be closer. Much closer.

Rowan could feel Molly's need in her kisses and saw it in her flushed face. She finished what Molly had started and pulled off her shirt and bra. She felt Molly working on the button and zipper of her pants.

Jumping from the bed, Rowan pulled her jeans and panties off at the same time. She grabbed the top of Molly's skirt, pulling it down her legs and off. She looked up at Molly lying in front of her, and she couldn't help the moan of longing that came out of her at the sight of Molly's beautiful body and her burning hazel eyes. "Oh, my god," she gasped as she put her fingers through the waist of Molly's panties and pulled them off with a smooth, fluid movement. Rowan crawled back onto the bed as Molly reached for her and pulled her close.

Molly gasped and pushed her hips up to Rowan. Her mind was swirling at the sensations that Rowan was causing. Every time she felt that sweet release coming, Rowan moved and took it away. It was the most frustrating bliss she had ever felt, but she was not sure how much more she could take before she had to beg Rowan to stop. But she did not want her to stop, ever.

"Never stop," she whispered as she gasped again.

At those words, Rowan's heartbeat quickened. The love that filled her heart came rushing out of her in every touch and kiss that she left on Molly's body. She didn't ever want to stop. If this was to be the last time she could show Molly how much she loved her, she wanted the memory of the love she was covering her with to last a lifetime.

She had loved Molly for so long, for all of her lives. But Molly may have to carry on in this life without her if they fail. Through her thoughts, Rowan felt Molly pulling her up and into her embrace.

Molly moved her hands over Rowan and the need to taste her lips filled her. Their lips met, and the taste made Molly dizzy. No one had ever made her feel this way. No one but Rowan. She felt Rowan move her kisses down over her breasts and stomach—down between her legs where Rowan's touches made Molly tremble.

"Oh, god!" she cried out as arrows of pleasure shot through her body, and Rowan pushed deep inside her. The sweet release that she had been aching for finally came, and she lost all control.

Rowan felt Molly's trembling body relax and heard Molly sigh, as she tasted the most wonderful taste in the world—Molly. She licked her and drank her in and then made her way back up Molly's body, leaving a trail of kisses in her wake.

She met Molly's lips as she pulled her close and kissed her breathlessly. Molly pushed Rowan back again and looked into her eyes. "Rowan, stay with me," she breathed. "Stay with me always."

Rowan looked back at her and into those beautiful hazel eyes. "I will," Rowan said. "I will, always. I want to so much."

She pulled Molly close, and they held onto each other tightly. They were swept into the warm feeling of love, and into a place where they so desperately wished they could stay together forever.

———————

CURLING A LOCK of Rowan's dark hair around her finger, Molly drank in her sleeping form. With her other hand, she ran her fingers over Rowan's forehead and down her cheek then over her beautiful full lips. *She was so soft, so kissable,* she thought as she licked her own lips.

Molly ran her fingers down over Rowan's chin and down to her neck. The feeling of Rowan's soft skin under her fingertips released a surge of tingling butterflies through Molly's body down through her core. Molly let out a short soft gasp at the sensation that ran through her. She smiled at the thoughts running through her mind, thoughts of all the things she wanted to do and share with Rowan. She moved her hand lower over Rowan's breasts and moved down her body. She was surprised when Rowan put her hand over hers and held it tight against her.

She looked into Rowan's liquid eyes and smiled. "Hi," she said and sweetly kissed her.

"Hi," Rowan replied softly as she pulled Molly's hand up and kissed it. "We have to get up. We have to break the seal and read Jessie's letter."

Molly put her head against Rowan's forehead. "Just a little longer." She swallowed and breathed in Rowan's perfume. "I want to make love to you."

Rowan pushed Molly onto her back and hovered over her. "We have to get up. Come on," she said as she kissed Molly quickly and hopped out of bed.

Holding onto Rowan's arm, Molly groaned. "No. Come back. It's my turn now. I want you."

Rowan pulled her hand away and smiled as she quickly dressed. "I owe you," she quipped and headed for the door. "Come on."

Molly watched Rowan walk out the door and frowned. "She, owes me? What the hell?" She jumped out of bed and threw on her clothes. She was feeling hurt and suddenly, cut off. "What the fuck just happened?" she wondered under her breath.

Chapter 24

ROWAN SAT AT the kitchen table looking at Jessie's letter and running her hand through her hair. She was not sure she could take this loss again. *It was just so unfair*, she thought—just when she found her again, she had to lose her.

She touched Jessie's letter in wonder. It was amazing to her that Jessie was able to speak to her from the past. In all the years she had spent searching, this had never happened before. She remembered their last night together and sighed. Now Molly will be going through the same thing. *How different would things be*, Rowan wondered, *if they could both have all the memories that only she had?*

"Rowan, what's wrong? Why did you go like that?" Molly stood over Rowan with her hands on her hips waiting for an explanation.

Rowan looked at Molly and thought, *why could I have just not met her? No. She was the one.* The one she would love forever no matter what. They were meant to be together. If only they could break this curse. She pushed the letter to the middle of the table.

"Molly," she hesitated. "What if we fail?" Rowan looked at Molly sadly. "Again." *Molly would have to go on and live*, she thought.

"Fail?" Molly asked with uncertainty. "Then we try again. But we won't. We have the letter from Jessie. This time will be different."

"What if it's just like all the rest. I've left them all behind, Molly, and now I may be leaving you behind, too." She looked at Molly and wondered what it was like for her, for all of them, to live a life knowing their soul mate was gone. "You should try to find someone—" she started.

"Stop it!" Molly yelled. She struggled with her anger and gained control of it as she saw the pain in Rowan's face. She took Rowan's chin into her hand and pulled her head up to look into her eyes. "Please, don't give up now," she pleaded softly. "We have something we've never had before. Jessie worked so hard and gave her life to get it to us, to you. This time will be different."

"But, if we don't…" Rowan said hesitantly. She pulled away and looked down so that she didn't have to look into Molly's eyes. "Look what it did to Jessie. Instead of moving on and finding some happiness, she died fighting this curse. Did she die unhappy? I'll never really know." She looked back up at Molly. "Will you do the same? I can't do this knowing you won't be happy."

Reality cracked like thunder in Molly's mind making her speechless. This was the reason for Rowan's sudden change. Molly could see now that in her own mind, she had created a false reality. She buried, for the short time they were together, the reality of what was going to happen. Rowan didn't bury it. Rowan couldn't. When they break the seal, what she experienced in her car will come down on them one hundred fold. When they break the seal, it might be Rowan's death sentence. An icy chill ran through Molly causing her shiver. She looked at Rowan sitting at the table with her head hanging down and her shoulders slumped in sadness. She put her hand gently on Rowan's back.

"Wait. I'll be right back."

Rowan looked up and saw Molly head for the front door. She unlocked it and walked outside. Rowan got up to follow Molly. She looked out the door and saw the sun bowing to the night. *Sundown,* she thought. *It would be starting soon.* She looked for Molly and saw she had popped the trunk of her damaged car and was taking out a cardboard box. Molly walked back into the house quickly with the box. Rowan frowned trying to understand what Molly was doing.

"What's that?" she asked as Molly made it to the door and stood in front of her.

Molly looked at Rowan with a spark of fear in her eyes. The trip to the car just added to her anxiety. "Let's go inside, and I'll show you." She made her way past Rowan and headed for the kitchen with Rowan close behind her.

Molly dropped the box on the table and quickly slid its lid off. She searched through the box. "I know it's here," she mumbled.

"What?" asked Rowan. "What are you looking for?"

"Ah! Here it is!" Molly took out a small leather bound notebook. "This is all of Jessie's notes. I put them in this box to make things easier to carry around because I've been working on the screenplay whenever I get the chance. I like to keep all this research material close just in case." Molly flipped through the notebook.

"Molly, we really don't have time to go through all of this now. We have to—" She did not get to finish her sentence as Molly interrupted.

"I have it!" she exclaimed. "Sit down and listen to this." She looked at Rowan who hesitated. Molly nodded her head toward the chair, and hesitantly, Rowan pulled out the chair and sat. "I want you to listen to this. It's something Jessie wrote, and I think—no, I know I feel the same." She looked at Rowan and saw her swallow as she waited for Jessie's words.

Molly read from Jessie's notebook.

"Before I met Lou, I felt like my life was routine, mundane. When she came into my life, it seemed like, for the first time, I could see color and beauty. I was suddenly awake.

"The year we had was like a wonderful dream that I never wanted to wake up from. When Lou died, I thought my world had come to an end. The pain was so severe, I was sure my heart would stop beating, and at any moment, I would take my last breath. But that wasn't what happened. I lived on.

"Then one day, it seemed like she was in my life again. I got her last letter. She found me and saved me again even though she was gone. I found purpose and happiness again because she showed me that even death couldn't keep us apart. She will be back, and so will I. I knew I never had to worry about losing her because I never would. We will always be connected. Always.

"Realizing this truth made my heart fill with joy and gave my life purpose. We will meet again. We will be together again.

"The greatest joy in my life now comes from making sure the next time we meet we will have that life together she yearned for so much. Giving her this gift is the least I can do for what she gave me. She gave me a life, a very happy life.

"The search for the clues to break this curse has taken me all over the world. I've met wonderful and interesting people. I've had a very adventurous life. I have had a full life. My life and happiness are all because of Lou. This work I am doing is a thank you… No, it's more than a thank you. It is my way of telling her that I love her. I will always love her. It is my way of telling her that I know we will be together again someday, and I'll be ready. Ready to live a lifetime with my true love."

Molly looked at Rowan and saw the liquid forming in her eyes making them shine under the lights. "I'm ready for that too, Rowan.

I am ready to fight for us, for a life together. I want it so much. I love you so much."

Rowan gripped the edge of the table with a strength she didn't know she had. Her knuckles were white and her body was tense. She trembled with the effort to let go of the table. Slowly, she stood up. It took a moment for her to remember how to walk. Hearing Jessie's words from Molly's mouth had stunned and shaken her. She slowly walked to her office and picked up the manila envelope from her desk. She turned back and walked toward Molly in a daze. *This is it,* she thought. *The sun is gone. The time was here.*

Standing in front of Molly, she put the envelope in the box with Jessie's things. "If," she started, "if I don't, I wanted you to have that for your screenplay. For—" She couldn't ask. She couldn't tell her she hoped it would help break the curse.

"Rowan." Molly sighed and put her arms around her. "Rowan, no matter what, I'll work to break this curse. I am Jessie. I am Evelyn. I understand that. I know we're meant to be together. I'll do whatever it takes."

Rowan held Molly tight and breathed her in. She looked into her eyes, and the soul she would always know. Moving her head down, their lips met and love flowed through them, binding them and filling them. Breaking away, Rowan ran her hands over Molly's body for what might be the very last time.

"It's time then. Time to break the seal."

———

KNEELING IN THE circle that Rowan made earlier with powders and chalk, Rowan and Molly looked at the letter that was lying between them. The pumpkin that was sitting next to Rowan, the one for her heart, reminded them of what the end of this night might bring.

"I think it will be safest to open the letter in the circle," Rowan explained as she took the pendant from her pocket. "You should put the pendant on now," she said as she slipped the pendant over Molly's head.

Molly had some of Jessic's notebooks beside her, and she touched the pendant that was hanging from her neck. "Maybe I should open it." She looked at Rowan who looked doubtful. "I think I should. I mean, technically, as we said before, I wrote the letter—as Jessie. So I put the seal there. And I've cracked it. So it makes sense that I should break it the rest of the way."

Rowan was hesitant but saw the determination in Molly's eyes. "Okay."

Molly picked up the letter and ran her finger over the corner where the paper was separated. She revealed a thin knife she found in the kitchen and slipped the tip between the edges of the pages. Rowan showed her surprise only by raising her eyebrows.

Very carefully, Molly pulled the top layer away from the lower layer using the thin knife to help separate the stiff pages. Outside, darkness fell like a curtain, and they heard an echoing thud. With eyes wide, they could tell one of the pumpkins had exploded because the light that was coming from it was gone. There was no doubt the demons were surrounding them and fighting to make their way inside the circle. Molly's hands shook.

Rowan took a deep breath and gave her a nod to continue.

Slowly and carefully, Molly separated the pages from each other taking care not to tear or cut either page. A bead of sweat ran down the back of her neck as she held the separated pages and looked up at Rowan.

"It's done," she said shakily.

Outside another light went out as a second pumpkin was destroyed. "They're coming fast," said Rowan. "Hurry and read it."

Molly held the page before her and looked at the handwriting on the page. It was nothing like what was on the other page. This writing was uneven and sprawling. Like the writer was fighting to put ink on the page. Molly took a deep breath and read the letter aloud to Rowan.

My Dearest Lou,

It is my hope that this last message from me will help us be together for a lifetime…finally.

Remember the riddle you had told me before you died? I hope you've been able to figure it out because, I think, though that part came first, some of it may, in fact, have to happen last.

The cost has been high but, incredibly, I have been able to add to it. I know my quest has not been in vain. I know it will help us break this curse. Use it well. Here it is…

'But only if the gift, the moon, and the sacrifice have made full circle.'

When the demons come, you must fight them… but this time, you will have to fight harder because they will know that this may be their end because you have more of the answers to the riddle.

At midnight, the 'one' will come. He is the one that was there at the beginning. Remember, for him and the others, this is a game. Something to entertain them, and now he is growing tired of this game even though, it seems, others don't want it to end. He must come. He has no choice because it is part of the game. To end this game, he must witness the gift, the moon, and the sacrifice as it must make a full circle for the curse to end. I'm not sure what it all means as I have had very little time to work it all out. But if you are to break the curse, you must figure it out before he leaves.

All I can say now to help you is the key is in understanding the curse and its beginning. The curse began with love. Love is unconditional. Love is big and deep and has more facets than a jewel. It is a jewel that must be given freely as it is most powerful when it is returned.

I desperately hope you or my future self will understand what to do. I can say no more…they are here. I don't want to compromise the work I have done and hidden from them. I must make the seal to hide this letter.

I love you from the beginning until the end.

Jessie

———————

MOLLY LOOKED UP at Rowan. "What was it?"

Rowan shook her head at what she had just heard. "She's rambling. It makes no sense!" She rubbed her hands over her face. "All this for nothing."

Looking up from the message, Molly put her hand on Rowan's arm. "She worked so hard. It has to make sense somehow. What was it you heard before you died?"

"It's the riddle," Rowan explained as she sat back on her heels. "She's talking about the riddle. Just before I died, I heard it. It said, 'Love's blood encased in flesh, you must fight all that come, and the one at midnight to reunite, survive twelve, thirteen and half of fourteen, and the life that was taken shall be restored and gain back its mortal time.'"

Molly looked at the letter again. "So to that we add… 'but only if the gift, the moon, and the sacrifice have made full circle.'" Molly looked at Rowan. "What does it mean? Do you understand it?"

Rowan shook her head. "No! Damn it! This is so fucking frustrating!" She took the letter from Molly to see the words with her own eyes. As she looked at the struggling handwriting, she was overwhelmed with distress at what Jessie must have suffered to write these few lines. Outside, a third light went out as the circle of pumpkins was attacked again.

"Okay. Let's try to be calm. Jessie said the key is in understanding the curse and its beginning." Molly picked up one of Jessie's notebooks. "What happened at the beginning? What happened with you and Evelyn?"

"You know what happened, Molly. We met at the cabin, and your fiancé came. He came, and he shot me. That's when it all started." Rowan's anxiety was growing. There was no way to figure this out now. No time. *We should have broken the seal sooner*, she thought.

Molly flipped through Jessie's notes. "Okay. Okay. Well, let's start with what we know—the first part of the riddle. Do you think you have it figured out?

Rowan threw up her hands. "I just don't know, Molly. I've tried so many different things, and none worked. Now I have to add this part. It feels like I have to start all over. Any of the things I tried before could have been right but didn't work because I didn't have this part of the riddle. I, I just…" Rowan stammered feeling all of the work she had done over her many lives had been in vain.

Molly could see Rowan's frustration and also felt a bit of her own as she blew an errant hair from in front of her face and looked through Jessie's notebook. She snapped it closed and sighed. "We have to look at this logically. Take it piece by piece. Jessie said the key was the beginning, so let's start there." Molly got up and walked out of the circle and into Rowans' office area.

"Where are you going? We need to stay in the circle where it's safe," Rowan said as she stood at the edge of the circle. She held in her frustration and fear that Molly just didn't understand the danger of their situation. "Hurry! Come back in the circle, Molly."

"Sorry," she said seeing the panic in Rowan. "I needed some paper and a pen so we can work this out." She stepped back into the safety of the circle.

"Well, just... just don't do that again. Please," Rowan pleaded. The sound of another pumpkin bursting into bits came from outside, and its candle went out. Rowan was too uneasy to sit and paced around the circle, instead.

Molly sat on the floor and placed the letter, journal, and paper in front of her. She tapped the pen against her chin as she looked over Jessie's letter again. If she could dissect it, maybe she could understand everything Jessie wanted them to know. She picked up a blank sheet of paper and began to write. When she finished, she looked up at Rowan who was still pacing around the circle and watching the pumpkins outside. Another one had been destroyed.

"Rowan, Rowan, sit down. We need to think about this now and concentrate. I have it all organized so maybe it will be easier to find the answers we need." She handed Rowan the paper she had been working on.

Love's blood encased in flesh, you must fight all that come, and the one at midnight, to reunite, survive twelve, thirteen and half of fourteen, and the life that was taken shall be restored and gain back its mortal time, but only if the gift, the moon, and the sacrifice have made full circle.

Love's blood encased in flesh = Rowan?

You must fight all that come and the one at midnight to reunite = fight the demons?

Survive twelve = Midnight?

Thirteen = Time between midnight and one? 12+1=13??

And half of fourteen = 7 mystical number, 7th hour, 7 days of mourning, 7 heavens, 7 oaths. Time? 7 hours, min, sec?

And the life that was taken shall be restored and gain back its mortal time = Rowan's life?

But only if the gift = ?

the moon = ?

the sacrifice = ?

have made full circle = ?

The key is in understanding the curse and its beginning = Evelyn and Lucas

The curse began with love = Began when Lucas was killed?

Love is unconditional.

Love is big and deep and has more facets than a jewel.

It is a jewel that must be given freely.

It is not a promise. It is not a vow. It is not limited to one lifetime.

It is simply always there.

It is most powerful when it is returned.

I love you from the beginning until the end.

———

SEEING THE RIDDLE and Jessie's letter broken up still did not help Rowan to see the answers they needed. Now it just made the problem look bigger and more complex. She sat down across from Molly and sighed as she handed the paper back to her. "I feel…" She ran her hands through her hair. "I feel more lost than ever now. Everything has changed."

Molly looked at Rowan and could see her despair. "Rowan, it's okay. You thought you knew everything, and now you're finding out that you don't. You shouldn't be disappointed, though. You should be happy that we're now closer to the answers we need. Besides, I think Jessie was right. We have to do this together. You've been trying all this time to do everything yourself." She put her hand on the notebooks beside her. "It seems like, in every life, you have been the protector and the guide while in all my lives, I seem to have been more of a bystander, except Jessie. But she didn't get to talk to you about all of this while you were together. This time, I know I'll be more than a bystander. And I have you here now to work things out with me. This time, we have a much better chance of succeeding. That is a change for the good."

Looking at the determination in Molly's face Rowan couldn't help but feel pride and love for the woman in front of her. Over the years, she had felt the failure was in her abilities, not realizing her failure might have been in trying to do everything alone.

She smiled and nodded her head in acceptance. "Together," she agreed. "We'll do it together."

Chapter 25

TIME WAS SLIPPING by quickly as they worked on finding the answers to the riddle. Outside, more pumpkins had been destroyed, and only two were left to protect them. Molly added a note to one of the many papers surrounding her. Rowan sat with the pumpkin in her lap toying with the dried stem.

"Well, I think you may be right about the gift. It has to be the pendant, and since you have given it to me already, that part of the riddle is solved," announced Molly as she made a check mark on the paper.

"Yes, and I gave it to you freely," Rowan added. "It seems like that's what Jessie was talking about with all of those lines about jewels. I don't know why she would have to tell me that, though. It's your protection. There's no need to tell me to give it to you freely."

"Right," Molly said as she took a mind clearing breath. "So we have that part and the time except for the half of fourteen. Do you really think it has to do with time? I know I argued about the thirteen, but it seems there are too many things that have to do with time. Maybe it means seven of something. Maybe seven more demons come."

Shuddering at the thought, Rowan shook her head. "No, I'm sure we have to deal with those first. When we're successful in fighting them, they are always gone at midnight." Rowan looked at

Molly as she concentrated on her notes. "It won't be easy, to fight the demons. I just want you to know that. But we've made it through before, and I know we can again."

Looking up, Molly bit her lip in concern. "I know." She looked down not wanting to think about what was coming yet. She shuffled her notes and sighed. "I don't know, Rowan. Something just doesn't feel right."

"Feel right?" Rowan asked in confusion. "Molly, we have been over this. We have a plan, and we both know what we're supposed to do. We don't have time to waste here. What exactly doesn't feel right?"

"I don't know. It's just something. I can't explain it, and I know it's frustrating. It is to me too. I keep reading Jessie's letters and her notes, and it feels like we are missing something that should be obvious." Molly ran her hand through her hair and sighed. "I just don't know what it is. But this nagging feeling just won't go away."

Rowan rubbed her temples and groaned. "Let's just think about the next parts for now—the moon and the sacrifice. I'm worried that the moon may mean a certain kind of moon. Maybe it's a full moon or quarter, or we may even have to figure out what the moon was doing on the night the curse began. It may have to be the same."

"To figure that out, we will need your computer," Molly said as she looked toward Rowan's office.

Rowan sat up straight, and her eyes were wide as she followed Molly's gaze out from the protective circle. "We can't, Molly. Not now." Her fear was supported by the sound of another pumpkin exploding, and its light dying in the night. Only one left. Rowan looked at Molly and could see the fear in her eyes. "Okay. Sacrifice. Let's talk about what that can be. The moon may just be another reference to time."

Swallowing back her anxiety Molly nodded her head slowly. "Sacrifice. If it needs to come full circle do you think it's a reference to your death?"

"Well, if it is I have been making that circle for a very long time." Rowan sighed. "But I don't want to..." she hesitated, "to die again. I want to live. I want to have a life with you. I want this curse to be over."

Molly took hold of Rowan's hand and squeezed it. "I want that too. So much," she whispered.

"It's what it must mean," said Rowan with a shaky voice. "I can't think of anything else it can be."

Molly looked thoughtfully at the pumpkin that was now sitting beside Rowan. She picked it up and held it in front of her. "Maybe it has to do with this," she guessed. "Maybe, since you are connected to it, maybe it's what needs to be sacrificed."

"I don't know," said Rowan with a troubled voice. "If something happens to the pumpkin," she shook at the thought, "I may not have a way to come back. There will be nowhere," she said softly, "nowhere for my heart, my soul, to go."

Setting the pumpkin down gently, Molly nodded her head. "True. So where does that leave us?" Molly's heart was beating hard as she looked at the pumpkin, her mind reeling at the thought of its importance. Without it, Rowan might never come back. Then they would never have a chance to be together. *How could such a small thing be so important to their happiness?* she thought. She was startled out of her thoughts by the sound of the last pumpkin that protected them being destroyed.

"This is it," Rowan declared. "They'll be here any minute now. Are we ready?"

Without a word, Molly nodded and climbed to her knees. She moved in close to Rowan, and they held onto each other for what might be the last time. She looked into Rowan's eyes and couldn't look away even as tears filled her own. "I love you. I'll always love you," she whispered.

"I love you too, always," Rowan said as she pulled her into a deep and loving kiss. She broke away hesitantly and put her head against Molly's forehead. "They're here."

Chapter 26

ALL HALLOWS' EVE, a night of mystery, demons, spirits, trickery, and magic—the night when the veil between the underworld and this world is at its thinnest. It was on this very night, so many years ago, a curse began. A night that was still haunting the souls it was cast upon. Since then, for the souls that now reside in Rowan and Molly, it had always been a night of challenge and heartbreak.

Inside the circle that had been carefully formed and lit up by candles, Rowan and Molly awaited their fate. The air surrounding the two souls grew thick as they clung to each other with love and determination.

Surrounding them, pushing against them, seeking out their weaknesses, the demons entered the circle. They moved along their skin feeling the life that they could never really have and left traces of their power that burned and stung. They entered into the minds that had no choice but to allow them in. They battered and weakened them.

The demons knew that even if they did not destroy these cursed souls, the chance of them defeating the One and solving the riddle was slim. It was a game they had enjoyed for many years though they were compelled by the curse to come and play. Being this close to life was addictive and exciting for them. They awaited their chance to play with life with great anticipation.

As the burning and prickling sensations moved over Rowan's skin, she braced herself by lowering her head and squeezing her eyes shut. The memories flowed through her and filled her mind. Each life flickered by quickly like a reel of movie clips. She laughed inside her head. *Molly would like that for her screenplay*, she thought. Then, just as quickly, the humor left her as she saw the pain in the eyes of every soul that Molly had been.

She stole a look at Molly and saw she was flushed and weakening. She looked up at the clock and saw that it was almost midnight. Not much longer. She put her mind back where it was supposed to be—on her love for Molly and the life they wanted to live together. She felt Molly weaken in her arms, but she held her up and held her close. "Not much longer," she told her. "Hang on, Molly. Hang on."

Rowan never knew what Molly's soul went through when they were fighting the demons. She had never had the chance to ask, never thought to, really. She knew it was hard. She knew they were relentless. Over the years, Rowan had learned how to hide and take the pain. But Molly didn't have the luxury of that knowledge. Rowan could feel the demons weakening. They were falling away slowly. The time was getting closer. Time for the One to come.

Rowan felt Molly shudder in her arms and go limp, her weight bearing down on her. "Molly?" Rowan opened her eyes again to look at Molly and saw she was ashen. "Molly! Oh, god!" She looked up at the clock, and it was seconds until midnight. "Molly! Molly!" She pulled Molly around to hold her in her lap and pushed her soft blond hair out if her face. "Molly, what's wrong? What's happening?"

Uncertainty filled Rowan as she looked down at Molly's lifeless form. She pulled Molly close so she could feel her breath and could feel that she was still breathing. She didn't have to look at the clock because she knew the time by the sound of the chime that began to ring… It was midnight. She rocked with Molly in her arms, her heart filled with fear and grief. "Molly. Molly, please wake up. I don't know what's happening." Tears streamed down Rowan's face.

Was this too much for Molly? Was she going to be okay? *Oh, god,* she thought. *Things aren't happening the way they have before.*

"I love you, Molly," she whispered over and over again. Leaving the circle could mean death for them both. Holding onto Molly was all she could think to do right now and wait for the one to come for them.

———————

SPIRALING, DOWN, DOWN, down into blackness, pain, and anguish, Molly felt herself dying. Doubt, fear, and hopelessness filled her soul, and it pressed her deeper into the dark that surrounded her.

"This one is weak," a small voice whispered. "She won't even survive the thirteen, let alone live to forget it all."

"No," replied another harsher voice. "Look at her fight. She may surprise us yet. This one may be more fun than the others have been. See that spark in her? It is growing, and it seems she is aware of more than the others."

"I see it, but it's still small yet. It could go out," said the smaller voice hopefully.

The voices echoed in Molly's head as she struggled to hear more. With a surge of will, she opened her eyes, but it made no difference. The darkness that surrounded her was complete. She tried to speak, but her tongue was heavy and her throat dry.

"We should help her," echoed a third voice. "We don't want to have our fun end too soon."

"No, don't," lashed out the harsher voice. "She has to come to us on her own. She has to survive the thirteen without our help."

"True," agreed the small voice. "We don't want to anger the One."

Hearing the voices move away from to her, Molly fought to follow them, but the way out of the darkness was too far. *I have to survive*, she thought, *for Rowan.* She knew she had to follow them to find out what they meant when they talked about the thirteen. Her head pounded as she felt the pressure of the darkness press against her, squeezing her, making it hard to breathe. *I'm dying, I'm really dying,* she thought. Panic began to build inside her as pressure pushed her body into a ball, and she spun deeper into the timelessness of the dark.

———————

MOLLY SAT UP in a fright, her heart beating hard in her chest. She looked around with confusion at the unfamiliar room she was in. *Where am I*, she thought. She looked down and knew she was in some unfamiliar bedroom, some unfamiliar bed.

Carefully, she climbed out of the bed and onto the cool rug. She looked around the room for some kind of a clue that would tell her where she was and what was happening to her.

The room was large and looked to Molly like it was decorated in a very antique fashion. One part of the room looked like a small sitting room with a polished table and cushioned wingback chairs framed by heavily brocade curtains that were pulled open to let in the outside light.

Near the ornate bed, there was a wardrobe cabinet, a washstand with a beautiful pitcher and bowl set, and a small vanity with a mirror. As she passed by the small vanity mirror, she gasped at the reflection. The reflection wasn't her. She turned to see if someone else was in the room. Nobody. She looked in the mirror again and carefully touched her face. This was not how she remembered herself. *How could this be,* she thought, not believing her own eyes. "Who am I?" she asked aloud to an unfamiliar face with pale blue eyes.

A sharp rapping on the heavy door startled Molly out of her confused thoughts. The door opened as she turned to face it. A frowning woman in a very plain, long, dark blue dress entered the room briskly and looked Molly up and down.

"Well, I see you have decided to finally get out of bed," the grim lady quipped with disapproval. She placed a letter on the vanity next to Molly and then made her way to the bed. She spoke quickly as she straightened the blankets and pillows. "I can tell by the handwriting who that letter is from, and I'm telling you, it will come to no good. How can you encourage such a thing? Shame! Your father will never approve of a… an artist!" she spat out with distaste.

"Artist?" Molly asked in confusion, but the woman seemed to ignore her and continued with her work around the room. Molly picked up the small envelope and saw the name written on it. *Evelyn.* Molly shook her head in disbelief. "I'm Evelyn?" she mumbled to herself.

"Yes, that's right. The note is for you, and it is from that man," snapped the frowning woman. She finished dusting and stopped to straighten her dress and apron. "I shall leave you to get dressed on your own today, and I shall send Cook up with a tray." She looked at Molly and the letter. "Mark my words, Ms. Evie—that will come to no good! No good!" She nodded her head to emphasize the rightness of her words and bustled out, closing the door behind her.

Molly trembled as she sat down in a large wing backed chair and looked at the small envelope again. "I'm, I'm Evelyn," she said out loud to herself again.

She knew she must be dreaming, or this had to be part of what happened when the demons came, but she was still shaking with fear of the unknown. Hesitantly, she broke the wax seal on the envelope and removed the card that was inside.

Evelyn—The colors of the oak leaves are beautiful in the fall, and you must take the time to enjoy them. They await your pleasure in the garden, as shall I—until I finish my painting.—Lucas

"Lucas." The name rolled off her tongue, and her heart leapt in her chest. The door opened suddenly, and Molly hid the card and envelope under her leg as a small woman with a tray made her way into the room.

"Hope you 'ave not been waitin' long, deary," she said sweetly as she sat the tray on the table beside Molly. "I see she 'as left ya on yer own to dress. Well, tha'll ne'er do. Eat up!" she gestured to the food. "I'll sort out somethin' fer ya."

"Thank," Molly hesitated, "you." She looked at the food and picked a thick piece of bread with butter and jam to eat. It tasted like heaven. She watched the small woman open the large wardrobe and pull out dresses like Molly had only seen on movie sets. They were over-run with lace, bows, ties, and buckles. Then she saw the corset and almost choked on her bread.

She brushed the crumbs from her hands and went over to the pile of clothes. She knew that she needed to take charge of the situation because there was no way she was going to be strapped into a corset. "I think I can manage," she said in a soft and unfamiliar voice. "I want to be comfortable today when I go for a walk in the garden."

The small woman looked at her and then smiled. "I understan' miss. Jus' don' let *her* find tha ya'v gone out wit'out dressin' proper or we'll both of us be in fer some troubles." With a wink and a curtsy, the small woman headed out of the room and with the click of the latch, Molly was alone again.

By the time Molly got dressed, she was sweating and flushed. Getting dressed alone in those clothes was a real workout. No wonder it took a team to get dressed. With so many loops, ties, and buckles, she felt like she was dressing in a strait jacket. She was sure she would need one if she had to go through this again.

She looked in the mirror at her outfit. "Not bad," she huffed and blew a stray hair from her face.

Sitting down at the powder table, she opened and closed several small pots. She had no idea what they were or if they would make her break out. *Wait,* she thought, *I'm Evelyn, not Molly.* Still, she didn't risk it and instead, ran the brush quickly through her hair. She picked up the long cloak she found and put it over herself. She hoped that if she were too improper, the cloak would hide her mistakes.

Picking up the card from Lucas, she turned and headed out of the only place that was familiar to her at the moment. Making her way through the house, Molly found her way to the front door easily. She quietly slipped out and headed into the garden to look for Lucas.

AFTER TAKING LUCAS'S clue and looking for the colorful leaves of the oak tree, Molly finally found him. He had not noticed her yet, and she stopped so that she could see him. Her curiosity was at its peak. Rowan got to meet her in so many different lifetimes, and now this was Molly's chance to see Rowan as someone other than herself.

Lucas was tall with dark hair. His chin was square, and he had very full lips. Molly couldn't tell what he looked like full on yet because she could only see his profile. He was sitting on a folding stool holding a small paintbrush and applying paint to a very small canvas that was held up by an easel. He was concentrating so hard he still hadn't noticed she was watching him.

Hearing a sound beside her, Molly gasped and almost let out a shout but managed to control herself. Before her eyes, leaves from the forest floor arose and formed into the shape of a small gnarly body.

"What are you waiting for? You're wasting time!" the small form complained.

Molly stared at the little thing but couldn't speak. The sight froze her where she stood.

It pushed against her leg with a grunt. "Go on then! This is the beginning. You need to keep going if you want to make it 'til the end."

Molly stumbled noisily out of her hiding place, and when she looked up, she saw that Lucas had turned to greet her. He stood, smiled, and walked toward her. Molly's mind whirled, and her heart raced. He was standing in front of her, and she was looking into his eyes. Rowan's eyes. In them, she saw love, joy, and kindness. Her world suddenly seemed right and safe and perfect. This was the person she wanted forever. This man, Lucas.

"So, you have finally decided to get out of the house, I see." He smiled as he teased her. "Did the old maid hold you up with her lecturing and scolding?"

Molly just looked at him in wonder. "Oh, no," she said as she regained her senses. "She, she did make me dress myself, though."

The most wonderful sound of laughter left Lucas's throat and his lips curled into a beautiful smile. Molly looked at him closely. She could see it. She could see Rowan reflected on him.

"Are you all right, Evie?" asked Lucas as Molly stared at him. "You act like you have never seen me before."

"Oh, I've seen you. I know you," Molly replied softly.

Lucas looked into her eyes, and his heart skipped a beat at the beautiful sight. "I love you, Evelyn. I love you with all of my heart and soul."

Molly opened her mouth to speak, but Lucas put a finger over her lips. A tremor ran through her body at his touch.

"Please, do not say a thing. Come, I have something for you." He pulled Molly along to his canvas and paints. He picked up his jacket and took a box out of the pocket and then turned back to Molly.

A prickling sensation ran down Molly's spine. In a blink of her eye, she found herself on the outside looking in. She could see Lucas approaching Evelyn under the large oak. Molly looked around in confusion. "What just happened?"

"Just watch," said the small form beside her as it rubbed it's dry and cracking hands together. "It is beginning."

Molly focused her attention on the two people before her. She saw the way they looked into each other's eyes and the way they struggled to keep from touching each other. She watched them, knowing she was a part of the love that passed between them as they spoke.

"Evie," Lucas started as he held a small box in his hands. "I want to give you something." He opened the small box in his shaking hands and took out the pendant. It hung spinning from a thin silver chain, glinting in the light. The colors in the stone seemed to shiver and change as Evelyn watched it sway. "It is a moonstone," said Lucas with a smile. "It's said to be magical, and it is called the stone of lovers. It is supposed to bring forth feelings of tenderness," he smiled, "and to protect true love. Love like ours." He looked around him at the trees and the sky then back at Evelyn. "I want to tell you here, in front of man, nature, and the spirits that my heart, soul, and love are only yours now and forever. I give this to you freely and unconditionally." Putting it over Evelyn's head, he spoke in a halting voice. "This is all I have to give you. I hope you'll accept."

Evelyn stopped him short with a tearful embrace. "Oh, Lucas! I do love you, and I do want to marry you!" she exclaimed then closed her eyes and kissed him.

Lucas hesitated, but he could not resist her or bring himself to tell her that they may never be able to marry. He could not bear to take away her moment of happiness. As they kissed, the wind picked up the fallen leaves sending the leaves tumbling over and around them.

"It's done," announced the gnarled form next to Molly as it clamped its hands together.

Darkness closed in around Molly's vision.

———————

PUSHING THROUGH THE cold darkness surrounding her, Molly ran through the soft leaves that blanketed the forest floor. Her body moved of its own accord as her mind had no idea where she was or how she had ended up there. She could feel the heat of her anger coming from her chest as she ran. Her cloak billowed around her as she stopped at the small wooden door and unlatched it to enter the cabin.

She made her way inside the cabin. The light of the moon helped her find the tools she needed for lighting a fire in the cold hearth. The fire came to life quickly and dried the tears on Molly's face, but it was still not as hot as the anger that burned inside her heart—Evelyn's heart.

After lighting the lamp with a small flame from the fire, she placed it on the table and went back to the hearth for warmth. She saw a small pumpkin across from her and was reminded that tonight was All Hallows' Eve. The servants had decorated the grounds including this small cabin. They were probably all happily gathering around the bonfire now. They could have their happiness. She was in misery. The thoughts of her father's arrangements for her marriage boiled into anger and heartbreak.

"I will never marry him!" Molly heard herself rage to the flames. "Never!" The pain in her heart caused tears to flow from her eyes again. "I would rather die! Die!" She raged. "Curse them and their arrangements! I am not an arrangement!" She looked into the dancing blue flames then at the pendant she held in her hands. "Protect me! Protect us! Please! I have to be with Lucas!" she cried. "If you're real like our love is real, you will not let this happen!" she pleaded and broke down into sobs of sorrow and grief. She dropped the pendant on the hearth.

"Evelyn? Oh, Evie, I came as fast as I could," Lucas said as he rushed into the cabin.

Molly stood and felt Lucas's sweet embrace, but only for a moment because she was pulled away by a burning hand. She looked around and saw Evelyn and Lucas embracing. In the hearth, she saw a fiery face with eyes of never-ending darkness. It looked at her with those terrible eyes, and she trembled as fear ran through her body.

"Watch," was all the crackling voice said to her.

Molly looked at Evelyn and Lucas, then conquering her fear, turned back to the face in the fire. "We have to help them. Lucas is going to be shot," Molly warned. "We have to stop this from happening," she pleaded.

"Watch," was all the face in the flame replied.

Molly struggled with her frustration and inability to help them. To help herself, she realized. "Hurry, you have to leave!" she shouted, but they had no idea she was with them.

They broke their embrace, and Lucas held Evelyn by the shoulders. "You're out in your nightgown, and you have no shoes. Evie, what are you thinking? You'll catch your death!"

"I don't care. I'm fine," cried Evelyn. "I wore my cloak." She looked up at him through her tears. "Lucas, take me away. Take me away tonight. Please," she begged desperately. "I don't want to marry him. I can't. I love you!"

As Lucas folded her in his arms, the cabin door opened and slammed with a jarring force into the wall.

"So what the maid told me is true then! Get away from her!" a booming voice demanded. "She has been promised to me, you fiend! I will kill you both!"

Molly watched in terror as the large form in the doorway lifted a long gun and took aim. She watched as Lucas pushed Evelyn behind him to protect her.

"No!" Lucas shouted, but it was too late. His voice was cut short by the report of the gun.

Molly watched as the shot traveled through the room and spread out in the air. Hundreds of tiny pellets slammed like a single fist into Lucas. Molly watched as some of the pellets furthest from the center entered and then exited Lucas and hit the hearth and pumpkin behind him, leaving traces of his blood where they had stopped.

"No!" Molly cried out as she tried to reach out for Lucas wanting to help Evelyn carry his weight to the ground.

"Lucas! Lucas! No!" shrieked Evelyn as Lucas fell against her and to the floor. "Help! Help me!" she screamed.

As Evelyn's screams faded, another form appeared in the doorway "My god, man! What have you done?" shouted Evelyn's father.

The gunman turned and looked at Evelyn's father then back at the twisted form of Lucas. He said nothing as he turned and ran out the cabin door.

"Come back! Murderer!" Evelyn's father shouted as he followed his daughter's murderous fiancé and called for more help.

Evelyn turned her attention back to Lucas. She held him close and kissed his face paying no attention to the blood that was covering her skin and white nightgown.

"Please don't die. It will be all right. Don't die, Lucas. Father will get help," she said as tears ran over her blood-spattered face.

"Evie," Lucas managed to whisper. "I love you."

"No!" Evelyn cried. "You cannot die! I love you! I love you! Help me! Someone, help me!" she screamed at the top of her voice. She held onto Lucas as tight as she could hoping her strength would keep him with her. "Oh, spirit of death, don't take him. Let him live, I beg you," she said in a desperate and pleading voice.

Anguish ran through Molly's entire body as she witnessed Lucas's death and Evelyn's grief. She knew this was her grief too, and it cut through her like a jagged blade. She reached out to them and yearned to touch and comfort them, but she was held back by the darkness.

"Watch," the crackling voice repeated, burning through her pain.

Molly watched as smoke filled the cabin. It gathered together and formed itself into an inky mass. It swirled and folded in on itself until it was molded into a towering dark figure. Its features swirled and changed, never staying quite in focus or solid. The one thing that stayed in place was the glowing red eyes. The smoke that surrounded them could not hide the eyes and their ominous glow. They were large orbs that seemed to be able to see in all directions at once. They were unwavering and unblinking.

Evelyn looked up at the demon with defiance. "You can't take him! I won't let you!"

The demon laughed, making Evelyn's blood chill. "You demanded help from the spirits. I am answering your call. But I warn you, it may be worse than death if I do."

"Help him! Help him, please!" Evelyn pleaded. "I love him."

"You have been duly warned," the demon replied. He picked up the pendant and the pumpkin from the hearth in his smoky hands. "This moon shall ever connect you." He placed the pendant on Lucas's bloody chest and held the bloody pumpkin before him. The demon waved his arm over Evelyn and Lucas. "Love's blood encased in flesh, you must fight all that come and the one at midnight to reunite, survive twelve, thirteen and half of fourteen, and the life that was taken shall be restored and gain back its mortal time, but only if the gift, the moon, and the sacrifice have made full circle."

Molly watched as Lucas writhed in pain and cried out. She watched as Evelyn wiped a tear from her bloody face then looked down at Lucas, her eyes wide with the sudden horror of understanding.

"No!" Evelyn cried in long moaning whale.

"It is the only way. This body is ruined," stated the demon without emotion.

Lucas grabbed Evelyn's hand and held it in his death grip. "I love you. I'm yours forever." He cried out in pain as the demon reached in and ripped his heart out of his chest and plunged it into the pumpkin.

The scream that was deep inside Evelyn did not make it to her lips. She trembled and fell over Lucas with her own heart bursting with pain.

The demon's inky form broke apart and turned back into dark smoke that flowed over Evelyn and Lucas. "When next we meet, you will remember me. Each life, I will remind you of this time and give you the thirteen. If you survive, and you can remember, you will have the life that was taken. Your strength will be tested, and your love will be tested. If you cannot find them, you will live forever in this moment."

Molly remained silent, the image of Lucas dying still fresh in her mind. She could feel Evelyn's searing pain because it was her own. She was in shock. She was in anguish. She was in torment. She was in pain. She was weak. She felt herself falling into darkness again, but this time, she didn't know if she ever wanted to come out.

"It is done," said a small voice in Molly's ear. "The One will be pleased."

Chapter 27

THE ECHO OF the last chime announcing midnight was ringing through the house. Rowan held onto Molly's limp form, watching the tears run out of her closed eyes and down her cheeks. "Hold on, Molly. Hold on," she whispered into her ear. "I love you." She wiped the tear from Molly's ashen face and rocked her gently. "I need you to come back. I need you to wake up, Molly. The One is coming. I can feel it. We need to do this together, remember?" Rowan's worried voice asked. She wondered if Molly would make it. There was no real way to prepare her for fighting the demons. It took strength of will, and if it weren't there, they would fail.

Molly began to shake and take deep, anxious breaths. She moaned in sorrow as her eyes fluttered open. She cried out in relief as she sat up and wrapped her arms around Rowan so tight she could barely breathe.

Rowan brushed Molly's hair from her face and looked at her with concern. "Welcome back. You made it," she said. "I was so worried about you. I know it'll be hard, but you have to get up now. The One will be here any second."

"The One?" Molly asked with a cracking voice.

"Look there!" Rowan whispered as her heart skipped a beat. "The One is here! Come on, get up." She pulled Molly to her feet and held her up.

Molly was feeling weak and confused. She felt like she had been drugged. Her vision was blurry, her mouth was dry, and she was very dizzy. "I think I'm going to be sick," she announced to the spinning room.

"Just breathe, breathe deep," Rowan told her as Molly bent over and held her knees. "You can do this, Molly. He is coming. Are you ready?"

Molly nodded her head as she took deep breaths and held onto Rowan to steady herself. She felt like she had been beaten down both physically and mentally. Her body ached, her head throbbed, and her mind was in so much turmoil she didn't know whether to laugh or cry. She could hear Rowan asking her if she was ready if she was okay, and all she could do was nod her head and hope she really was ready.

Without warning, a burning pain shot through Molly's body taking her to the ground. She pulled Rowan down with her as she cried out. She could feel Rowan grip her tighter in her arms, and she wanted to tell her to stop, but she couldn't seem to speak. She felt Rowan's breath against her ear, and she struggled to hear her.

"I love you. I'll always love you. Our love is strong. It's strong enough to survive this test. We can do this together. Our love is true. I'll never stop loving you," Rowan repeated over and over again and willing her strength to Molly.

"I—" was all Molly could push out of her lungs as a dark inky smoke surrounded them.

Large orbs of never ending darkness appeared before Molly's eyes, and fear gripped her as a deep laugh filled her ears. "Do you remember me?" it asked, without really expecting an answer. "It is time for the thirteen." The demon growled and reached out a smoky tendril that touched Molly's head. It moved over her and then to Rowan while surrounding them with darkness.

More darkness, thought Molly as she closed her eyes against the pain. Slowly, she became aware of faint flashes of light around her. They seemed to be moving in on her, getting closer and closer. She was not sure if she should be afraid or not. She was not sure if she had the strength to get away from them even if she should be afraid.

They moved closer.

The light was all around her now, and she could hear the echo of many voices in her ears. She remembered Rowan whispering that she loved her. "I love you too," she said not knowing if it was out loud or only in her mind.

"Are you sure?" asked a distant voice. "You must not love it enough. You never keep the thirteen in your mind. You never remember. Your love is not true."

"It is!" Molly yelled back in anger.

"You don't even know him, her, it, this time. You have doubt, uncertainty. So this love is not true."

"No! You're wrong!" Molly lashed out. "My love is true. I know it. I did have doubt and uncertainty. But that was about myself. Not Rowan!"

"Is that what you call it now? Rowan?" the voice laughed. "So many names, so many years. How is it that you're so certain? Or will this be like the other times where you proclaimed your love but never find the strength to remember in order to end this game?"

"This is not a game! It will end this time! I will remember!" Molly shouted in anger at the mocking voice.

The demon laughed, and a flash of golden light cut through Molly's mind. Memories and words coursed through her mind filling her and coming alive, touching every nerve in her body. Torment, ecstasy, agony, pleasure, pain, she felt it all. Her ears were filled with sounds—thousands of sounds. Her senses were overwhelmed with scenes from long ago memories. Memories flooded into her of making love, of loss and pain, and memories that she never had in this life but, in reality, she had always carried with her. Memories of Lucas blended with memories of all his other lives and with Rowan.

Rowan.

The demon took hold of Molly's mind again. She willed herself to think of only one thing. Rowan. Rowan was waiting. Rowan needed her to be strong. Rowan was whom she loved. Rowan. The golden light went out, and she was left empty again.

"I have given you what you need as always," the demon announced. "Remember and begin again. Forget and we carry on."

"Molly!" Rowan exclaimed. She loosened her embrace around Molly and watched as she opened her eyes. "It's okay now. It's stopped. Now we just have to figure out the rest of the riddle."

"Rowan, I…" Molly whispered as she wiped her hand across her eyes. "Something happened."

"I know," Rowan said. "I know. We made it! We survived, that's what happened. We have a chance now to break the curse." She helped Molly sit down. She could see this had been hard for her. *But she made it,* she thought happily. She made it again. Her heart filled up with love, and she couldn't help smiling and kissing her. "I love you. I love you. I love you," she said as she kissed her gently.

"I love you, too. So much." Tears broke away from Molly's eyes. "I had the strangest dream."

"Your dream can't be any stranger than our reality," Rowan said with a sigh as her joy was cut short at the sight of Molly's tears. "It's okay, don't cry. It's okay." She took a deep calming breath. She couldn't bring herself to tell Molly she wanted to get it over with quickly. That she wanted the pain that may be coming to end as fast as possible. She couldn't tell her she wanted to have time to say goodbye and kiss her one more time. Despair surged over her, and she stood up quickly and turned her back to Molly so she couldn't see the fear she knew was showing on her face.

Molly looked up at Rowan and knew there was something she should remember, but she just wasn't sure what. The demon. She jumped to her feet. "Rowan, we can't let him leave! Remember what Jessie said—he has to witness everything."

"I don't think he is leaving. He has to be here for when I step out of the circle or for when our time is up. He's here. Waiting," Rowan said as she looked around the room. She picked up Jessie's letter and Molly's notes. "We wait until one o'clock now I guess if your twelve plus one theory is right for the thirteen. We still have to figure out what the half of fourteen means."

"Thirteen," Molly whispered to herself. She felt a pulling and nagging in her mind. She knew there was something she had to remember.

Why can't I remember, she wondered?

Rowan's voice barely filtered through as Molly tried hard to concentrate, but no matter where she turned her mind, the feeling that she should know something would not go away.

Every theory they discussed seemed wrong somehow and the frustration was growing in them both. The chime signaled the quarter hour, and Rowan looked up at Molly. At that echoing reminder her heart jumped to her chest as the knowledge she may die again tonight stabbed into her mind.

Time was running out.

The midnight hour was almost gone. She looked at Molly chewing on her pen and concentrating. Her mind went over the short time they had together, and she hoped desperately they would have more time.

A lifetime.

"Molly," she whispered. "It's time. We have to decide now."

Molly looked up from her notes and blinked wondering how the time went so fast.

"Okay." She sighed. "Let's go down our list. We have the pendant that is the gift, the moon we have to hope just means night and the sacrifice—you." Molly gulped at the thought. "We have the pumpkin here. Now the half of fourteen is all we need."

Rowan nodded her head slowly. "I think I should try seven seconds again. Maybe it was right but never worked because we didn't have the last part of the riddle."

"Okay, seven seconds," Molly agreed and wrote it on the paper. "Rowan?"

"Yes," Rowan answered softly.

"Hold me, Rowan. I need to feel you against me again," Molly said to her through liquid eyes.

Rowan sat down next to Molly inside the circle that protected them. She kissed her deeply and ran her hands over her body. She felt her familiar form, her warmth, and her arms that encircled her neck.

They held onto this moment, the one that could be their last. They took comfort in each other's presence. Tenderness filled them, and the love that had been inside them for so long surrounded them. They were meant to be together. There was no doubt. Their love was true and strong.

There was no uncertainty.

They were together.

They were one.

———————

WITH A SIGH, Rowan kissed Molly and sat up on her knees. There was no need to speak. They both knew what was coming next. "I'm ready," said Rowan with an unfaltering voice.

Molly looked up at her and nodded. She laid out the pendant next to the pumpkin as Rowan watched. She placed the paper with their notes between them and looked up at Rowan.

With on final deep breath, Rowan began. She picked up the pendant and placed it around Molly's neck.

"The gift is returned," she said to the room knowing the demon was watching. She pointed to the window. "The moon is once again upon us, it has returned." She picked up the pumpkin. "The sacrifice is here and shall be made again with love's blood." She swallowed and looked at Molly's pale and frightened face. "All is done." She looked at the clock and stood up waiting for the clock to strike one. Waiting to take her first step into life—or her last step in this life. She moved closer to the edge of the circle.

"Wait!" Molly shouted and held her back.

"Molly, I have to go. It's the only way to know if it worked."

"I, I know," she said, as she ran her hand nervously through her hair. "It's just…just." She looked into Rowan's eyes and took a sharp breath, as her mind was suddenly clear and calm. She knew. She remembered. "Rowan. Rowan, do you trust me?"

"Yes, of course," Rowan answered in confusion.

"Step back," she said as she pulled Rowan back into the circle.

"Molly, what is it. What are we doing?" Rowan asked anxiously.

"Rowan, do you remember what Jessie said about her epiphany?" she asked as she looked at Jessie's note again. She looked up and saw Rowan nodding in confusion. "She had an epiphany, a sudden understanding, a moment when certain knowledge was just known or remembered."

"Molly," Rowan said as she shook her head. "I know what an epiphany is. I just don't understand what you are trying to say. We have to hurry."

"I know! I think. I think that's what the thirteen is. Thirteen is when knowledge is bestowed upon you. When you are allowed to know certain secrets and participate in certain ceremonies. I know we interpreted it as time, and it seems like a stretch here but... Rowan, I just had an epiphany! The thirteen!" She looked up at Rowan knowing what she had just said must have sounded crazy. "Trust me. Will you?"

Rowan's mind was buzzing with uncertainty. She didn't understand what Molly was talking about, but she knew she was on the brink of desperation.

"I trust you."

"Do you love me?" Molly asked.

"I do, with all of my heart," answered Rowan without hesitation.

"Okay, good. Take my hands." She reached out and grasped Rowan's hands. Flashes of Lucas under the oak tree glinted in Molly's mind. "Rowan, I want to tell you here, in front of man, nature, and the spirits that my heart, soul, and love are only yours now and forever. I give this gift to you freely and unconditionally."

Rowan began to speak, but Molly put her fingers over her lips. She reached for the chain around her neck that held the pendant and the iridescent jewel sparkled as it turned.

The moonstone.

The magical moonstone.

The gift.

Rowan tried to protest, but Molly slipped the pendant over her head and touched the moonstone. "The moon is returned," she declared.

Rowan shifted from side to side and touched the moonstone herself while Molly picked up the pumpkin and the knife that she used to help open Jessie's letter. The temperature in the room felt like it had risen and she began to sweat.

Holding the knife tightly, Molly set the pumpkin in the middle of the circle. Images of Lucas dying appeared before her. She saw images of the pellets with his blood hitting the pumpkin and entering it, leaving his blood inside. She looked up at Rowan and could see the horror on her face as she began to understand what was happening. Holding the knife steadily and firmly, Molly placed the blade tip in her hand. With a quick flick of her wrist, she cut into her hand and her blood flowed over the knife. "Life's blood encased in flesh," she said. "The sacrifice is returned." She plunged the knife tip into the pumpkin so that her blood entered it.

"No!" Rowan cried as she watched the knife descend.

Molly looked up as Rowan cried out and watched as Rowan began to turn pale.

The blood.

The binding force.

The sacrifice.

"Molly, what's happening?" asked Rowan as her chest tightened and she began to shake. "What did you do?"

Molly jumped up and stood with Rowan holding her ice-cold hands. "We've survived, Rowan. I know it. Life's blood encased in flesh. The sacrifice has been returned. We've survived twelve and the demons that came. We have been given the thirteen," she whispered, "the epiphany, and it has been remembered. The gift, your gift of love I have returned to you. I love you. The moonstone, the pendant, the moon that ever connects us has been returned to you. It has been returned to protect the true love that I have given you and that we have for each other." She squeezed Rowan's hands. "I know this is right, Rowan. I know it."

The chime on the clock struck one o'clock, and Rowan looked at the clock with wide and fearful eyes. "Half of fourteen! The last part!" she said as she turned away from Molly and rushed to the edge of the circle.

"Rowan! No!" Molly cried. "I have to tell you what it means! Stop! No!" she cried and reached out to stop Rowan from stepping out of the circle.

Molly watched as her hand missed Rowan's sleeve and she stepped out of the circle. She watched as Rowan turned to look at her with a pale smile, not realizing what was happening. She watched as Rowan's smile faded and tears of pain sprang to her eyes as she clutched her heart. She watched through her own stinging tears as Rowan crumpled to the floor and did not move.

She watched it all helplessly at seven seconds after one.

CHapter 28

THE WORLD WAS out of balance. There was no solid ground anymore. There was only loss, sorrow, pain, and grief. Where were the happiness, the comfort, and wellbeing? They were gone. No more. Extinguished. They had been spilled out of the world by a curse that had tormented the ragged and battered souls of Molly and Rowan for so long.

Everything was done correctly, Molly thought—*everything.* She sat in the dark going over every moment and every detail of that night. They fought the demons with all of their strength and held on to their love for each other through it all and survived the Twelve. Molly survived the Thirteen, the epiphany… She gained the knowledge of what was to be done, and she remembered everything. *Everything was done right,* Molly thought again to herself in the dark.

She gave her life's blood and returned the sacrifice. She declared her love, her true and deep love in front of nature, man, and spirit. By doing so, she returned the gift of love to Rowan that Lucas gave so long ago. She returned the moon as a token and protection of that love by putting the moonstone pendant around Rowan's neck as Lucas had done for Evelyn.

The only thing left to survive was the Half of fourteen.

"Half of fourteen," Molly whispered in the dark. She could see it all clearly in her mind. Rowan turning away from her, reaching out to catch Rowan's sleeve, Rowan's beautiful smile fading from her pale face, fading as her body folded down to the floor. *There wasn't time*, thought Molly. Rowan moved too quickly. She was not able to tell Rowan what it meant.

Everything was done right, she thought again.

Self-doubt crept into her mind. *Did I do everything right*, she wondered. *Maybe it was to be done in a different order.* Molly ran her shaking hands over her face as she thought about all the other possible choices she may have had. She shook her head pushing her doubts away as she looked at her stinging bandaged hand, the hand she had cut to make her sacrifice. She closed her eyes and tried to clear her head of the doubts that were crowding in on her. *I did everything right*, she thought. *I know I did.* There was only one thing that was left to survive.

"Half of fourteen," she whispered softly.

CHARLOTTE SAT IN her sisters' bedroom and looked around her. She realized that, for a sister, she knew very little about Rowan. She sighed at the thought of all she had missed in Rowan's life. She should have supported her when she decided to go to school for art history and not become the lawyer their father wanted. Instead, she left Rowan on her own with their father and moved to New York to work in a brokerage firm. Rowan left home and followed her to New York, but they barely saw each other. She should have helped her, should have been there for her. *Where does a person who has failed a person this badly, this miserably, go from here?* she wondered. All it takes is one late night phone call to make failure complete and unchangeable.

She remembered the hospital calling. She remembered rushing to email a medical consent form. She remembered giving them the name of Rowan's friend Amy and confirming that she could make decisions in her absence. Amy was really the only friend of Rowan's that she knew, and since she was on the emergency contact information, she knew that Rowan trusted her. If anything happened to Rowan or went wrong while she was on her way to the hospital, Amy could step in. Charlotte sighed again at that thought. She tried calling their father, but as usual, his work came first. She remembered the annoyance and distance in his voice as he told her that 'Rowan would understand.' She shook her head as a tear fell from her eye. They both had failed Rowan.

Charlotte closed her eyes and thought about the hours she spent getting to the hospital and not knowing what was happening to Rowan. She had never felt so helpless and afraid. She still didn't know exactly what had happened. She sighed and sat up straight trying to get herself together. She got up and walked over to Rowan's closet and opened the door. She looked at all of her sister's belongings and wrinkled her brow in concentration as she went through them. "There are more labels in here than in the kitchen pantry," she mumbled to herself. After gathering the items she needed, she fit them into a small case and headed out of the bedroom. She saw Amy sitting on the couch as she placed the small case by the door.

Amy sat on Rowan's couch and tried to think of her life without Rowan as her anger boiled inside her. She could not believe this was happening. Rowan. Dead. It could not be. *She should have come to the party with us*, she thought. Then this wouldn't have happened. *I should have insisted*, she told herself. But Rowan said she had some stupid mysterious plans.

She couldn't forget that night. The feeling that went through her body as she was told something had happened to Rowan.

Valoria's restaurant was filled with monsters, grizzly murder victims, witches, ghouls, devils, and princesses. There were a few rock stars and clowns in the crowd to round out the cast of characters. The music was loud, and the drinks were flowing. The dance floor was so crowded that personal space was not an option. Amy was making the most of the situation.

"I'm in the zone tonight!" She laughed. "I love this time of year!" She looked over at the scantily clad girl who bumped into her. "Oh, so hot!" she said and moved to dance close with the girl. "So, you like candy?" she asked the girl and laughed at her own joke.

Shannon shook her head at her friend's antics. She smiled at Amy in her candy corn costume as the song they were all dancing to ended. "I'm going to the bar. Thirsty!" she said as she pointed at her throat.

"Okay!" yelled Amy as a new song began and she turned her attention to her newest objective. "Even hell isn't as hot as you, babe!" she shouted and laughed again at her own drunken joke. She moved in for the kill and felt her phone vibrating in her pocket. "Aw, shit!" she said as she pulled it from her pocket. She looked at the number and didn't recognize it. "Hello!" she shouted over the music into the phone. "What?" she yelled. "What?" she asked again and went as pale as the cheesy Halloween ghosts that decorated the club. "No! No, I'll be there as soon as I can! I'm coming!" She hung up her phone and looked up to see Shannon not far away. "Shannon! Shannon, come on! We have to go. It's Rowan! Something's happened!" Amy yelled as she grabbed Shannon.

She could feel her heart slamming into her chest, and her body shook with fear. A sick feeling washed over her as panic took over her mind. They pushed their way through the bar and out into the cool Halloween night.

Amy swallowed back her pain and tears that the memory tried to draw out of her and looked up at Charlotte. "What the hell happened?" she asked as she got up and walked around the living room. "I mean," she sobbed, "did you see Molly's car?"

"Yes, I saw it," said Charlotte as she went to the kitchen and checked the refrigerator for things that might spoil.

"And look at the living room. It looks like World War Three hit it. What the hell were they doing?"

Trying to control herself, Charlotte just shrugged. "I don't know."

"Well, I think Molly finally pissed off Rowan. I think they got into a big fight. I mean why else would things be so messed up? I think Molly did something to Rowan. The police found a knife with blood on it and everything."

"Amy, I think the police helped make some of this mess. I don't want to try and guess what happened. The police will figure it out." Charlotte sighed as she gathered up the trash.

"It's all Molly's fault," Amy declared as she paced. "Who else's could it be? She was the only one here. I can't believe they haven't arrested her and put her away somewhere."

"Please Amy," Charlotte said as she tried to hold back her tears.

"I'm sorry. I really am. But I know it's her fault! I want to know exactly what happened. I just don't understand any of it."

"Me neither," admitted Charlotte. "Let's go." She headed to the door with the trash.

Amy followed. "I'll get the case," she offered, and she picked it up as Charlotte opened the scarred front door. She shook her head at the damage to the door and the broken out windowpane but managed to hold back from verbalizing her thoughts. "Shannon called. She's going to meet us there."

"That's nice," said Charlotte. Another friend of her sisters she never knew she had. Charlotte sighed as she felt the completeness of her failure press in on her.

———————

HALF OF FOURTEEN. Seven. Seven seconds, seven minutes, seven hours, seven days. Seven. The light spectrum has seven colors, the musical scale has seven notes, and the week consists of seven days. Seven.

Thoughts of 'seven' filled Molly's mind as she sat in the dark and looked at her hands. God rested on the seventh day. He was very tired, she supposed. After creating all that life, he must have been exhausted. What about her life? What about Rowan's life?

Half of fourteen, she thought. She had to be sure what it meant. She had to think it through and figure out what to do. Maybe she was thinking about it all wrong—*'chercher midi à quatorze heures,'* as her old French teacher would say. Maybe she is making the matter more difficult than it needed to be. Seven.

She looked up from her hands slowly. There it was. The white pillow. She hesitated and looked further up the pillow. There it was—that dark curl that she ran her fingers through not long ago. She swallowed and forced herself to raise her head to see more. There it was. The face of the person she loved with all of her heart. *She was so still,* Molly thought. *She looked so peaceful.*

"Half of fourteen," she whispered. She forced her eyes away from that still peaceful ashen face. She looked down until she saw a hand, a hand that had touched her, caressed her and made her feel so alive and loved. She reached out and touched the soft still hand. *It's so cold,* she thought. She picked up the soft cold hand and brought it to her lips. Softly, she kissed it. "I love you. I'll always love you. Always."

Half of fourteen, she thought. She went over everything again. She remembered her epiphany, and then she suddenly knew. Half of fourteen was not a time. Fourteen was *deliverance*. Only having to complete half of fourteen would imply that the first half was already done. *Something had to be finished,* she thought. What did they forget? She had to go over everything again. She had to remember before it was too late. She had to fight, and she had to be right. She had no idea how long the demon would make her fight or make her wait. But she knew nothing could make her leave Rowan right now.

Nothing.

Chapter 29

"SHE JUST SITS there," quipped Amy as she paced the hospital waiting room. "I ask her something, and she just says 'half of fourteen.' What the hell does that mean?"

"I don't know, Amy. Sit down," sighed Charlotte as she rubbed her temples.

"Give the girl a break. She's been through a lot," added Shannon, and Charlotte nodded in agreement.

"Give her a break? Give her a break? Now why should I do something like that!" she said angrily and kicked a chair. "She's killed her! Your sister is dead, and you want me to give Molly a break? No fucking way!"

"Amy!" Shannon cried as she jumped up from her chair in anger. "You don't know that! Don't say that!"

"I do know it!" Amy fumed. "Rowan tried to warn me, but I didn't see it!"

"Amy, please," Charlotte begged in a shaky voice, "this is not helping."

"Yeah, stop," Shannon growled. "Charlotte told me the girl has barely slept or eaten in days. She's not doing well herself."

"I don't care! I hate her!" Amy cried and then turned on her heal and fumed as she walked away.

Why should she give that... that bitch a break? She killed Rowan. Tears streamed down her face in uncontrollable waves. Rowan. *Molly should die too*, Amy thought—*no, she should have died instead*. It wasn't fair. Rowan was her friend. More than her friend. She loved her.

Charlotte held Shannon back from following Amy. "Let her go. She doesn't mean it. She is just hurting," said Charlotte softly. "We're all hurting."

"Who exactly is she?" Shannon asked as she sat down next to Charlotte. "I knew Rowan was seeing someone because Amy told me, but I don't know anything about her really."

Charlotte pulled an envelope from her purse. "Her name is Molly. Molly Gentry. Rowan wrote to me about her. She said she loved her, and she wanted me to always treat her like a sister."

"Wow. I guess she really liked her if she wrote to you about her," Shannon said with a raise of her eyebrows.

"Yeah, she usually isn't too willing to open up about those things... to me, anyway." Charlotte sighed. She looked up at Shannon. "You're a good friend, Shannon. Thank you for coming."

"No problem." Shannon shifted in her chair and looked down the hallway. "Someone's bringing more flowers," she commented.

"That's nice," Charlotte replied and wiped her nose with a tissue.

———————————

MOLLY COULD FEEL the air in the room move as someone entered. She closed her eyes and welcomed the darkness as she kept her lips against the cool hand she was holding. She shivered as the air moved over her, and she knew that whoever was in the room had moved closer to her. A low, angry voice filled her ears.

"I hate you," said the angry voice. "She loved you and you—you did this."

Molly could hear soft footsteps as someone paced in the room.

"She asked me to be your friend if anything ever happened to her. I am damn sure if she knew what you were going to do to her, she would never have asked me to be your friend."

Molly felt the person move close again. She felt breath on her ear.

"I will never," she fought down her anger, "never be your friend," whispered the voice hotly.

Molly felt air take the place of the whisper as it moved away.

"Why won't you tell us what happened? Why won't you talk to us? Say anything?"

Molly took a shuddering breath. "Half of fourteen," was all she could say as a tear fell down her cheek. She felt her chair move when an angry hand pushed it.

"That makes no sense! Stop saying it!" growled the voice. "She loved you. She loved you, and that is all you can think of to say!"

A soft sob escaped from Molly, and she put her head against the hand she was holding. It seemed to be soaking up the warmth from her. She would willingly give all the warmth she had if she could. *Take it all,* she thought. *It's yours. I'm yours. All yours,* she thought.

"You never loved her!" came that angry voice again. "I don't think you even know what love is, let alone have the ability to give it! If you really loved her, you would tell us what happened. Why she loved you is an absolute mystery!"

Molly felt the air as it flowed over her again and heard the echo of footsteps as the person left the room.

Love. *There is nothing mysterious about love,* she thought. It was a gift freely given but sometimes not appreciated for its value. Love was all around us, but some people would never see it, never feel it. Like many things, the gift can be abused and used by evil and unfeeling people. They use it to hurt. Love could be very painful.

People want it, lie about it, steal it, crave it, and do almost anything to get it. People even use it to cheat and trick. They want to deserve it, buy it, trade it, sell it, and some people even refuse to give it even when it is desperately needed.

It affects all of the senses. Love can be blind, make a person deaf, make a heart ache. It can be tasted and be brought out with a scent. Love can heal, make sick, and destroy lives and nations.

Mostly, though, she thought, *love is good.* It can be felt through art, words, and music. Love was in laughter, in tears, and even in the very air we breathe. It is all around us all of the time if we would just take the time to see it, recognize it, and then give it back. It is a gift that is always appreciated more when it is returned. It is what connects people. It's what brings people together and brings joy to those it touches. It connects us through time, and it connects us to the mystery of the spirits and world around us that we cannot see.

Yet the most amazing thing about love is that it can create—life.

Half of fourteen, Molly thought.

———

"SO HAS SHE been sitting in there this whole time?" asked Shannon, as she sat next to Charlotte in the waiting room.

"Just about. They had a hard time making her leave after she made it into the room. That's one strong girl. I told them to put a bed in there for her." Charlotte let out a short grief filled laugh. "They thought I was crazy, too. But then I pulled out Rowan's Will and Medical Directive. She's on it. So they finally let her stay."

"Do you… do you really think she is going to die?" Shannon asked holding back the emotion from her voice.

Charlotte shook her head sadly. "I just don't know. It's been a week. I just don't—" she broke down and couldn't stop her tears from flowing out again.

Amy walked quickly down the hallway wiping the angry tears from her face and then sat down hard in a chair beside Shannon. "She's still crazy," she announced angrily. "Still won't say anything helpful."

"Amy, why don't you calm down and leave her alone?" asked Shannon. "Give her a chance. Don't you think she is taking it pretty hard as it is without you harassing her?"

"I won't calm down! Every time I think about it, think about that night, think about the call I got, think about how the house looked," she hesitated to try to control the anger and the tears that threatened to burst out of her. "I won't calm down until I have some answers!"

Looking up, Charlotte saw the doctor speaking with the detective who was assigned to the case. They broke apart from their conversation and walked over to them.

The doctor was a balding man with dark circles under his eyes. The detective was a young woman with dark hair and was dressed in a nicely tailored suit. *She looked too young*, thought Charlotte. As they approached, Amy stood up and put her hands on her hips. The two barely made it over before Amy confronted them.

"When are you going to arrest her?" she asked hotly.

The detective looked confidently into Amy's face and then looked at her notebook. "Amy Wanden, right?

"That's right, and I want some answers!" she demanded.

"Well, Ms. Wanden, I have no plans to arrest anyone yet."

"What?" Amy stomped. "Why not? She's clearly the only one who could have done this to Rowan!" She looked at the detective suspiciously. "Did you even see the house?"

"Amy, please," begged Charlotte. "Let the detective talk."

"It's okay, ma'am." She reached out her hand to Charlotte. "You must be Charlotte Cortman-Meyers. I'm Detective Regis." She looked at Amy and back at Charlotte. "I understand that Ms. Wanden is upset, and I'll give you what information I can."

"Then you'll arrest Molly, right?" asked Amy with annoyance and frustration.

The detective cleared her throat. "No. As I said, I'm not arresting anyone yet. I am still trying to collect information and am waiting on results from the crime lab."

"What? Still? It's been a week! Haven't they got their results back by now?" Amy complained.

The detective shook her head. "This isn't a television crime show. We have more than two or three cases and things are a bit backed up."

"Well, what *do* you know?" fumed Amy.

The detective was undaunted and looked in her notebook. "Well, we have processed the knife we found. We know that the blood on the knife and in the pumpkin was Ms. Gentry's blood. That explained the cut on her hand." She looked up at Amy raising her eyebrows and then back at her notebook. "We also talked to Ms. Gentry's ex-boyfriend. He confirmed a confrontation that explained the bruises on Ms. Gentry's arm and possibly the condition of her car. However, he denies damaging the car."

"So it was Molly's ex who did this? In my book, it still makes this Molly's fault!" Amy said as she crossed her arms.

"Amy, please, you need to calm down," said Shannon, with concern. "Blaming Molly won't change anything."

"I can't believe you are all so concerned about Molly!" Amy growled to the detective. "What about Rowan? She is the one who's dying!"

"Ms. Wanden, I know this is hard, but there are no marks on Ms. Cortman. Nothing at all tells us that she was attacked." The detective flipped through her notebook and continued. "Ms. Gentry, on the other hand, has cuts on her face, hands, and feet as well as bruising on her arms and on top of her head. We have to look at where there is evidence of a possible assault or other crime."

The doctor cleared his throat and nodded to the detective who turned to Charlotte. "Ms. Meyers, I know this is difficult for you and your friends. The only thing we can tell is that your sister did suffer, what looks like, a mild heart attack."

"A heart attack?" asked Amy with suspicion.

"Yes, well," the doctor sighed and turned back to Charlotte. "Our concern is that the symptoms of a mild heart attack don't usually," he hesitated, "well, they don't usually cause a person to go into a comatose state or even just a state of prolonged deep sleep. She has brain activity, quite a lot actually, and all her vitals are normal," he said and shrugged his shoulders.

"So what are you saying?" asked Amy. "Did she have a heart attack or not?"

"Shh. Amy, stop," murmured Shannon as she saw Charlotte put her face in her hands in distress.

"I don't understand. If it wasn't a heart attack, what do you think happened?" asked Amy, ignoring Shannon.

The doctor shook his head sadly. "We just don't know. Her heart shows all the signs of being healthy. Electrocution possibly, but there are no burn marks," he sighed heavily, "not that there has to be."

"So what are you saying? She isn't going to die? She's okay?" demanded Amy.

The doctor held up his hands and shook his head. "I can't say that." He then continued in a very stiff and clinical voice. "Though she seems fine physically, she has failed several other tests. She is unresponsive to the pain of a pinprick and to the olfactory response of smelling salts. We can't be sure, but her excessive brain activity may be an anomaly, and there may actually be very little or no real brain activity. I'd like to do another test. If she is unresponsive, we will know," he hesitated, "we will know with certainty that she is gone. Braindead."

"Oh, fuck!" groaned Amy and sank into a chair next to Shannon. "I can't take this." She leaned her head on Shannon's shoulder and Shannon held onto her as she cried.

Charlotte sobbed and wiped her tears with a tissue. *This is not happening*, she thought. She gathered some control of herself. "When, when would you do this test?"

"As soon as you're ready," the doctor said stiffly. "I know you're letting Ms. Gentry stay in the room with your sister. We will have to move her. I don't think it would help her state of mind to be there during the test."

"I'll talk to her," said Charlotte. "I'll try to help her understand what needs to be done. She deserves to know."

Amy looked up at the face of the people deciding Rowan's fate. "How can you all have sympathy for her? She killed her! She killed Rowan! I know it! I know it!"

"Shhh, Amy," hissed Shannon trying to calm her.

Charlotte looked hotly at Amy and shook her fist with the letter from Rowan gripped in it.

"Amy, now Rowan has asked me to treat Molly like a sister. I am not going to disrespect her wishes for you or anyone else! Rowan loved Molly, you hear? She loved her, and you need to show some respect for that! If you can't, I don't know how you can call yourself Rowan's friend!" She stood up shakily and looked at the doctor and the detective. "I'm sorry. This is very hard on all of us. I'll go talk to Molly."

———————

CHARLOTTE OPENED THE door to Rowan's dark hospital room and quietly stepped inside. She saw that Molly had climbed into bed with Rowan again and that she had not eaten. She made her way around the room, moving the food tray, opening the curtains and rearranging the flowers so they were near the light and were all closer together so they would take up less room. She saw that Molly had put away the clothes she brought for Rowan.

She looked over at Molly and then Rowan, who was now in fresh pajamas. She saw that Molly was watching her. She approached the bed and rubbed Molly's shoulder.

"Molly, I need to talk to you. Do you think you can get up and come sit with me?"

Charlotte watched as Molly hesitated and looked at Rowan then nodded her head that she would come. "Here, let me help you." She helped Molly untangle from Rowan's IV tubes and monitor wires. She helped her sit up and climb down from the bed. *She is so small and frail,* Charlotte thought.

"Hon, you need to eat. Rowan wouldn't want you to get sick from not eating."

With Charlotte holding onto Molly, they took the short walk to the table and chairs by the window. Charlotte took Molly's hands across the table.

"Molly, I need to tell you that the doctors want to do another test on Rowan." She could feel Molly stiffen. "I know it will be hard for you, but they need you to leave the room while they do it." Charlotte looked at Molly's face and could see the horror and distress on her face. "I know you don't want to, but I think you should." She looked into Molly's tragic eyes but couldn't look for long. "Molly, the test," she swallowed, "the test will determine if Rowan is brain dead. They need to do this."

Tears streamed down Molly's face. "No," she said and shook her head. "Please," she said in a hoarse voice. "We just need a little more time." Molly squeezed Charlotte's hand. She knew she couldn't explain everything to Charlotte. She couldn't tell her what had happened. She couldn't tell her why they needed more time. She knew the doctors would never believe her, and they would make her leave. She couldn't leave. She had to stay with Rowan. "Please," she whispered. "Just wait one more day. Just one."

Charlotte watched Molly beg for more time with Rowan and her heart broke for her.

This girl truly loves my sister, she thought.

She cleared her throat and squeezed Molly's hand in return. "The doctor said they'd do it when we're ready. I think waiting one more day is a good idea," she said softly. "I think it will help us all, and it will give us time to say..." she hesitated, "to say goodbye."

"Thank you," said Molly as she slowly got up from her chair and made her way back to Rowan. She ran her hand through Rowan's dark hair and kissed her. "Half of fourteen," she whispered. "I did everything right. I know I did. I love you. We are running out of time. Please, please," she whispered and climbed on the bed and wrapped her arms around the motionless Rowan.

Charlotte watched as Molly made her way back to Rowan and lay next to her. She looked around the room not really knowing what to do next. She noticed Molly's untouched food tray again and sighed. She got up and walked to the hospital bed. "Molly, you really need to eat."

Molly shook her head and held Rowan closer. "Half of fourteen," she whispered.

Sighing and shaking her head Charlotte pulled the blanket up over the girls. "I don't know why you keep saying that, but it's driving Amy crazy." She watched Molly and Rowan for a few minutes and sighed. "They'll want to come in to say goodbye. I'll give you a while then I'll send them in. If you want…" she said sadly, "need to leave, it'll be okay."

She watched as Molly held Rowan closer and knew that she would not leave the room. She hadn't left Rowan's side for anything for seven days.

The door closed on Rowan and Molly, and they were alone again, alone to carry on with their fight for Rowan's life. "Half of fourteen," said Molly. "Not much longer. Please let this be right."

Molly had been watching over Rowan and reminding her of the love she had for her, reminding her of how much time had passed. Today was the seventh day. Today had to be the day they would find out if they were to live a life together or if they begin again.

SADLY, CHARLOTTE MADE her way back to where Shannon and Amy were waiting. They both stood as she entered the waiting room.

"Well? What happened?" asked Amy before Charlotte could sit down.

"Nothing happened. I just talked to her and told her what the doctor wanted to do," answered Charlotte not hiding her exasperation.

"Is she okay?" asked Shannon quietly. "Molly, I mean."

"She's holding up," replied Charlotte.

"Did she say anything to you? Anything about what happened?" Amy asked stubbornly.

"No, we didn't talk about that. We talked about what was going to happen with Rowan," explained Charlotte.

"So what did she say?" Amy asked again.

"She asked for one more day," Charlotte said as a tear leaked from her puffy eyes.

Shannon and Amy looked at each other and sat down slowly next to Charlotte as the words 'one more day' echoed in their minds.

"Shit!" Amy burst out with a squeaky voice as she tried to hold in her tears, and Shannon slouched down in her chair.

Charlotte took a deep calming breath and let it out slowly.

"I told her we would wait one more day. That'll give us all the chance to say goodbye."

She rubbed her temples and looked up at Amy.

"Amy, can you make some calls to let everyone know what's happening?" She watched Amy nod tearfully. "I told Molly I'd give her some time and then I'd start sending people in."

Chapter 30

MOLLY WAS SITTING in her chair next to Rowan's bed again. The people stopped coming in at regular intervals quite a while ago and visiting hours were almost over. All the while people from Rowan's life were coming and going from the room, Molly stayed as close as she could to Rowan. She sat in her own bed, or at the little table next to the window, or in the chair next to Rowan's bed. She refused to leave the room. No matter what they said, she would not leave. She could not leave Rowan. She didn't care about the whispers or if they thought her strange or disturbed. They didn't understand. They couldn't. They didn't know what was happening and why it was so important that she stay with Rowan. They didn't know about the curse.

"Half of fourteen," she whispered to Rowan as she looked closely for any sign of change in her, no matter how small. "It has to be today. I love you. Come back to me, Rowan. They have to let you come back. I did everything right. I know I did."

The heavy rain rapped loudly on the windows and brought Molly back from the memories that flowed through her mind, memories that spanned many lifetimes. She remembered. She remembered all of her lives now, just as Rowan remembered hers. The memory she had just thought of was the one of their very first kiss. Not that of Rowan and Molly or of Jessie and Lou. It was their true first kiss—Evelyn and Lucas. It was the kiss that would eventually lead them to this very moment.

"Rowan? Rowan, do you remember our first kiss?" she asked the still form before her. "I mean the very first," she said softly. "When we were brand new." She brushed her fingers through Rowan's hair. "When we were Evelyn and Lucas. It was summer, and you were teaching me to paint. You were showing me how to make the clouds look real. I could feel you close to me. The breeze was light, and wisps of my hair blew into your face. I turned and saw you looking at me with those eyes—those bright, beautiful, golden brown eyes. I lost all of my thoughts. My breath wouldn't come, and my heart was beating hard. You were very presumptuous." Molly smiled down into Rowan's still face. "You kissed me without asking. You never have to ask. Never. I love you." She kissed Rowan's forehead and smoothed the blanket over her.

Molly looked into Rowan's face again and sighed. There were so many memories, but they all ended so suddenly. All of their many lives she could see in her mind. They were all combined in her mind now. They were all here in front to her. They were all Rowan.

Over the past seven days, the memories had been filling her dreams and coming to her unexpectedly. When they came, she told Rowan about them in great detail. There were so many lives where Rowan tried to help them live a lifetime in only a year and so many where Rowan was not there. In all of those lives, when she could never find what she was looking for and never know who she was missing, she was missing Rowan.

"I'm so glad you found me again," Molly told Rowan as she kissed her cheek. She looked at her closely. She looked again. There it was. She was sure. Yes. She saw Rowan's eyes move under her eyelids, and they opened the tiniest bit. "Oh, my god," Molly whispered. "Rowan."

The air in the room dropped in temperature and Molly looked around her as she could feel a presence in the room. In her mind, she could feel a prickling and knew that the One was back. She could hear the booming echo of his voice in her mind. "Half of fourteen," he boomed. "It is time."

Molly held onto Rowan's hand tightly and stiffened her resolve as she was swept into darkness. She fell down into the black depths as her heart beat with fear. Slowly, strands of light began to weave their way through the darkness, and soon, she was able to see the stark world before her. The glowing eyes of the One appeared from the dark, and she turned to face the demon in her mind. She could see Rowan standing next to him.

"Rowan. Rowan, come back. Come and live a lifetime with me."

"Do you love this soul?" asked the demon.

"Yes," answered Molly without hesitation. "Please keep your promise and give her back to me. Let us finally spend a lifetime together."

"So you aren't satisfied with the memories that I have given you? Are they not enough to make up a lifetime? You have many," declared the demon.

"True," agreed Molly. "I do have a lot of memories now. But those memories don't add up to a lifetime. Our love is always in new bloom. There is never time for it to grow, for us to grow together."

"Ah," said the demon. "But new love, love in bloom as you put it, is the finest. It is powerful and has intensity like no other. Do you want your love to flower and then waste away? If it ends now, you will not have to worry about that. You will have these memories, and you will never see the love truly end."

Molly smiled. She knew what he was doing. He was trying to trick her. He was trying to keep them in his game. "Love never dies, demon. It never ends, and you know it's true. Love can change and grow. It can evolve and become even more powerful and intense. If it could die, we wouldn't be here at this very moment."

The demon scowled and squinted his dark eyes. "Love can do all of that. But what if this is not true love? What if this love does not evolve as you hope? What if the love you have for this soul evolves into love for another? Then what is this life worth? If that happens, this soul is better off here with me, never knowing the pain of losing the love it has fought for over the years."

Molly thought about the demon's words and rubbed her temples. She looked up at him and swallowed back her fear. "I love her. I don't want her to have that much pain ever."

"Good," said the demon. "We are agreed then. I will keep this soul."

"No!" Molly shouted. "No! There is a better way." The demon waited for her explanation. "Take away all of the memories. Take them away from both of us and let our love grow or evolve as if we had only known each other for this lifetime," Molly pleaded.

"That wouldn't be any fun." The demon laughed.

"I...we deserve this chance, this chance that was taken away from us so long ago and so terribly," insisted Molly

"Love is never deserved," growled the demon. "Nor are second chances at life, and that is what we are talking about."

Molly could see the anger ebbing around the demon as he looked at her. Fear shot through her and her breath came in short puffs, her heart beating loudly, and her mind racing. *What was happening,* she thought. *What am I missing?* she thought in fear.

"Demon, I pleaded for your help, and you gave it. You have kept this soul safe for many years. I now plead for its return." Tears sprang to Molly's eyes. "My love is true and tested. My strength has been tested, and I am still here." She hoped the strength she had left was enough. She had barely slept or eaten for days. She had been too worried about Rowan.

She gathered herself and looked at the demon again. "I survived the half of fourteen. I watched over the body so that it would not be ruined as the other one was ruined. Please," she begged. "Time is running out. They want to declare her dead tomorrow!" Molly implored as more tears fell. "I remembered everything as you told me to do, and I survived them, though many caused me pain and despair. Through these tests, my love has not wavered, and I ask you now to release the soul you have. Release the one I love and return her to this body. Return her so that we may live out our mortal time together until its end if it is our destiny."

Molly's head reeled as she tried to figure out what to do next. The demon seemed to be waiting for something, but she just didn't know what he wanted. *Half of fourteen was seven,* she thought. Fourteen was deliverance. Half of fourteen was seven. Seven was completion, perfection. She had to prove her love was true, and she had. She stayed with Rowan and never left. She proved her love was strong, and their love was perfect. She proved their love was worthy of saving. She was the one who had to prove her love was true to the demon and end his game. What more did the demon want from them? Half of fourteen. Something had been half done. What was it, she asked herself as her mind twisted in torment.

"She's not going to remember," said a small voice. "Let's begin this game again."

"No!" cried Molly. She had never made it this far before and now that she had she was not going to waste her chance. "I—," she said suddenly, "I remember everything! I remember the night of the curse and," she swallowed, "and my demand." A flash of realization shot through Molly's mind making her legs weak, and her heart beat hard in her chest. "I started the curse. I started it with a demand." She ran her hands through her hair and over her face. She had to complete the curse because she started it. It could not be done by Lucas or Rowan. She was the only one who could do it.

All this time, Rowan had been working so hard, and all the time it was only Molly who could break the curse. She started it with a demand. She would have to finish it with another demand. It was up to her to break this curse. She was the key.

"I demand what you agree, demon. I did everything right. Now the life that was taken shall be restored and gain back its mortal time! I demand it!" Molly shouted. "I demand that you give back the soul you took!"

Molly watched as the demon considered her words. Silently, she hoped for all of this to finally end for herself and for Rowan. Rowan. She saw her standing next to the demon motionless, frozen.

Was this where she had been the whole time, she wondered.

What had she been going through all this time? She watched as Rowan stiffly and slowly turned her head toward her. Their eyes met, and she could see the spark of hope that shined in Rowan's eyes. Molly's heart warmed, and she smiled—love and warmth bursting from her very soul.

———————◆———————

WITH A DIZZYING snap, Molly found herself looking down at Rowan in her bed again. She saw Rowan's eyes move again under her eyelids, and she smiled.

"What the hell are you smiling about? Happy about it all finally being over?" Amy growled from the doorway.

Molly looked up as Amy crossed to Rowan's bedside. She held back her excitement and her urge to call out to Rowan. *Oh,* she thought, *if I could only tell her how happy I am that this curse may finally be over.* But she couldn't. She just looked at Amy and didn't say a word. She found this was the best way to deal with Amy. If she couldn't argue, eventually she would storm away.

Amy looked at Rowan and took her cool hand. Her anger now lost to the sorrow that filled her for the loss of her friend. The loss of the woman she loved. She could not believe this was it. She couldn't believe that—Amy stopped thinking and looked up at Molly suddenly.

"She, she moved! Did you see that?" asked Amy, and Molly nodded at her with a smile again. "She moved!" squeaked Amy. "She's alive! I have to get the doctor! Charlotte! Everyone!" She ran out of the hospital room, and Molly could hear her yelling for help.

Molly leaned over Rowan and with happy relief, whispered in her ear. "Welcome back, my love. Welcome back. I missed you. I love you." She saw Rowan's brow furrow as she began to slowly come out of her deep sleep.

———————◆———————

THE ROOM BUZZED with activity. Doctors and nurses surrounded Rowan checking innumerable things and blocking

Molly's view. Two nurses approached her and pushed her away from the activity.

"You'll have to leave the room now," the first nurse stated to Molly.

"No!" Molly said defiantly and tried to push past them.

"Ma'am, it's best if you're outside to give us room to work," she said matter-of-factly.

"I won't. I won't leave," said Molly sternly as the nurses tried to take her by the arms to direct her out forcibly.

The doctor looked over and saw the desperation on Molly's face. He knew she had been at Rowan's side since she was admitted. His heart went out to her. *A rare thing,* he thought, *must be getting soft in my old age.* "Let her stay," he told the nurses as he examined Rowan. He saw the questioning look on the nurses' faces, and he shook his head. "I said let her stay."

Molly rushed to her own bed and climbed in. She had to stay close. She had to be in the room, close to her when she woke up. She watched as the doctors and nurses worked, and finally, one by one, they left. Only the doctor was left in the room. She got out of her bed and hurried over to Rowan's bed where she took her hand tenderly.

"I think she is coming around. It may be just a little longer, but it looks like she made it," he said as he filled out a chart.

The door opened, and Amy rushed back in the room. "Charlotte and everyone is on their way," she announced. "I saw everyone leave the room. How is she?" she asked the doctor.

"She seems to be fine. Maybe it was electrocution after all," he said shaking his head. "This has been a very strange case."

A groan came from the bed, and they all directed their attention to Rowan. Her eyes fluttered, and her lips moved. Slowly she opened her eyes. She squinted, trying to bring the world into focus, and had to close them again because the light seemed so bright. She tried to speak, but her throat was dry.

"Hey," said Molly. "Here's an ice chip. Go slowly." She gave Rowan a small ice chip and watched as Rowan literally came back to life.

The demon had released her. They had finally won. Molly could not stop smiling. She didn't know if she would ever stop.

Amy leaned over Rowan from the other side of the bed. "You're going to be fine. Maybe you should hire someone to change your light bulbs from now on!" she said with annoyance.

"What?" Rowan croaked out softly.

"You really need to stay away from anything electrical. You're lucky Molly was there."

"Who?" Rowan said with confusion. "Molly?" she asked and tried to open her eyes again.

"Oh fuck! Don't tell me you lost your memory! This is too much!" Amy said as she threw her hands up in the air.

"What's going on?" asked Charlotte, as she breathlessly entered the room.

"Memory's gone," Amy explained to Charlotte. "She doesn't know you now," she said to Molly with some satisfaction. "She's a blank slate now. I'm telling you, the mind and electricity don't mix well."

The doctor interrupted Amy's diagnosis. "It may just be temporary. Nothing to worry about. We see it a lot in cases like these. She should be back to normal soon."

Charlotte walked over to Rowan with concern on her face. "Rowan? Do you know me?" Rowan looked into Charlotte's face with blurry vision and confusion.

"What about me?" Amy asked as she pushed herself in front of Charlotte. "It's me, Amy."

"Who?" asked Rowan still confused and rubbing her eyes still unable to see clearly.

"Give her some time," said the doctor. "She probably just has some disorientation at the moment."

"Come on, Amy," said Charlotte as she pulled Amy out of the room. "Let's go tell everyone she's going to be okay."

"Rowan, it's okay," said Molly squeezed Rowan's hand. "You don't have to know anything right now."

Rowan turned her head toward Molly's voice and her vision cleared. She looked into Molly's hazel eyes, and her heart jumped as she took a sharp breath. Her head spun, and a feeling from deep inside her shot its way through her body like electricity. She watched Molly smile. *That smile*, she thought. "I know I love you," she said breathlessly and rubbed her forehead. "I know I owe you something."

Molly's eyes twinkled as she smiled and remembered their last bedroom conversation. "Yes, you owe me."

Rowan looked intently into Molly's sparkling eyes, and her heart skipped a beat as waves of love washed over her. "I owe you a lifetime. That's all I have to know. Is it over?" Rowan asked softly. She watched Molly tilt her head slightly to the side and wrinkle her brow.

Understanding came to Molly, and she smiled. Rowan wanted to ask about the curse. She still had her memories. "Don't worry. Everything will be okay." She moved closer to Rowan's ear. "I guess right now I know things you don't know," she whispered. "I think that's fair."

Rowan smiled at Molly who seemed to be glowing. She had so many questions, but she knew they would have to wait. Her heart soared knowing she was still here, knowing she was alive and with the person who she loved so deeply. She reached out and touched Molly's face to make sure she was real.

The pull of love overwhelmed them as they were drawn together.

The world around them faded away as their lips met.

They became lost in that single moment of pure love that connected them and had kept them coming back for each other for so long.

They finally knew they would be together for a lifetime.

They knew their love would last… this lifetime and beyond.

~ fin ~

Other Books by C.L. Cattano

An Epic Lesbian Romance Serial

Salvaggio's Light

Book One
SHATTERED PARADISE

C.L. Cattano

Join the Journey…

About the Author

C. L. CATTANO lives in the Midwestern U.S. with her partner and their dog somewhere between the city and the forest. With a joy for traveling, she and her partner have visited many countries and have a love for meeting people and learning about the places they visit. When possible she likes to include references in her work about the things she has learned, the places she has been and people she has met while on her travels and in her everyday life.

Cattano has a variety of creative interests including, but not limited to, creating art, writing, riding her bike, and throwing huge lesbian parties. She also enjoys spending time with friends and working for LGBT community service projects. She considers herself a 'Jack of All Trades' dabbling in what she terms the 'whimsies of her soul' that pull her toward happiness and fulfillment.

www.ingramcontent.com/pod-product-compliance
Lightning Source LLC
Chambersburg PA
CBHW051528280626
47161CB00022B/2852